Elevator in Sài Gòn

ALSO BY THUẬN

Chinatown

Thuận

ELEVATOR IN SÀI GÒN

translated from the Vietnamese
by Nguyễn An Lý

A NEW DIRECTIONS
PAPERBOOK ORIGINAL

Originally published in Vietnamese as *Thang máy Sài Gòn*
by Nhã Nam & NXB Hội Nhà Văn
This edition is published by arrangement
with Tilted Axis Press and Astier-Pécher Literary Agency.

Manufactured in the United States of America
First published as New Directions Paperbook 1607 in 2024

Library of Congress Cataloging-in-Publication Data
Names: Thuận, 1967– author. | Nguyễn An Lý, translator.
Title: An elevator in Sài Gòn / by Thuận ; translated by Nguyễn An Lý.
Other titles: Thang máy Sài Gòn. English | Elevator in Saigon
Description: New York : New Directions Publishing Corporation, 2024.
Identifiers: LCCN 2024009046 | ISBN 9780811238540 (paperback) |
ISBN 9780811238557 (ebook)
Subjects: LCGFT: Satirical fiction. | Ghost stories. | Novels.
Classification: LCC PL4378.9.T57493 T4713 2024 |
DDC 895.9/2234—dc23/eng/20240325
LC record available at https://lccn.loc.gov/2024009046

2 4 6 8 10 9 7 5 3 1

New Directions Books are published for James Laughlin
by New Directions Publishing Corporation
80 Eighth Avenue, New York 10011

Elevator in Sài Gòn

1 Sài Gòn

My mother died on a night of torrential rain. A night of unseasonal rain in 2004. In such a freak accident that our language probably had no word to name it. Mai, my brother, my only brother, had just constructed for himself yet another multistory house, this time with a home elevator, said to be the very first in the whole country. Such a momentous event called for celebration, so he bought my mother a plane ticket to Sài Gòn. Only after her inaugural push of the elevator button—he insisted—only after her round from the ground floor to the top and back, could his guests avail themselves of the device. Among said guests even were members of the press, print as well as TV. Such events always followed a predictable script, but I still spent the evening after my mother's funeral watching a sixty-minute DVD and flipping through a hundreds-strong album of photos of the inauguration, and then another sixty-minute DVD and another hundreds-strong album of that day's funeral, which I had attended from start to finish.

I'd realized at a very young age that my mother had always been something of a standout, whether alone or in the middle of a crowd, at a party committee meeting or one for the local civil unit, as a recipient of a certificate of merit or bestower of a prize, and now, on the family altar, she was a standout among the dead, her dead, her parents and in-laws and elder siblings. And her husband. My brother had taken care to put their portraits side by side, nestling behind a vase of red roses, but they still looked like two strangers who'd never signed a marriage license, never lived together for two decades, never birthed two children (my brother Mai and me) who gave them two grandchildren (Mai's daughter Ngọc and my own son Mike). That evening, I tried and tried to evoke a family scene from our former life, but in vain; I could picture my mother's face clearly, but had to refer again and again to my father's portrait, wreathed by red roses and thick incense smoke. He had died ten years earlier.

We had dinner together, my brother and I and the two children. Mai said, "Those inspectors from the German elevator company looked into every corner they could but couldn't pinpoint the cause of the accident. The elevator worked perfectly well during the inauguration, perfectly well for the next three days, and perfectly well after the accident, so they simply couldn't comprehend how the car could have stayed stationary down below, oblivious to her call, when Mother fell into the shaft, all the way from the top to the ground floor. And I can't comprehend what on earth Mother could have been doing on the top floor at such an hour, in such rain, for such a long time."

He gazed at me intensely as he said this. I felt like what he meant to say was that it wasn't the rainy season, not even close, but what he said next was, "As I recall, I'd been lying on the sofa since early in the evening, I watched a beauty contest and then fell asleep, Ngọc was at her mother's, the help had all gone home for the night, and even if the live-in housekeeper went upstairs to clean she would have retired to her room by nine, as she always does. And she said as much to the inspectors when they interrogated her, which was confirmed by the fact that the elevator was on the ground floor, where her room is. So, the sequence of events is as follows: Mother took the elevator to the top floor before nine, then the housekeeper took it to return to the ground floor, then at around two a.m. Mother called the elevator to go down, the doors opened, and she walked right into the shaft. The accident happened at two a.m. The coroner had confirmed that the time of death was two a.m. So what could Mother have been doing from nine p.m. to two a.m. on the top floor?"

I said nothing. I too was baffled as to what my mother could possibly do on the top floor from nine p.m. to two a.m. What can you do on a top floor from nine p.m. to two a.m.? What is there to do on a top floor from nine p.m. to two a.m.?

"Madame fell from the top floor to the ground floor, the body was a wreck, only her face was intact."

That's all the housekeeper had to say to me about the accident. Presumably she didn't know much else because, as the coroner concluded, the accident had occurred at two a.m. when everybody was fast asleep. But two a.m. or whichever a.m., there was no changing the fact: my mother was gone. And I couldn't help but visualize the way she'd fallen from the top floor to the ground floor in that dark, tunnellike space. And I suspected that during the fall, she had tried her best to keep her face upward, and wrap her arms around her head to protect her face, at the price of a more drawn-out death, the terrible pain of which her brain would have tasted for several minutes before the end.

According to the housekeeper, moreover, the wreckedness of my mother's body had required the tailors and funeral house staff to work for three days nonstop, while the makeup artist only needed a little over an hour. When I finally got in, her face was already properly made up, powdered and mascaraed, the way she never was in daily life. Her body, clothed in a black brocade áo dài and surrounded with red roses, lay in a glass coffin, with AC and odor-controlled, housed in the funeral wing of a famous international hospital. Only when everything had been done to perfection did my brother let the guests in, from whose number I was not excepted. In truth, my protests were only perfunctory. I wasn't eager to behold a wreck of a body, my mother's or anyone else's. My imagination was at least more lenient. But maybe that's why, seeing her in her glass coffin, wholly intact, with the brocade dress and the red roses, the powder and the mascara, I was struck by the impression that she was only playing dead, and I didn't shed a tear. And tears would be incongruous in that oh so clean and elegant funeral house, amid the attentive and beaming staff, after crossing a door above which a sign, in both Vietnamese and English, advised that the Esteemed Guests Please Refrain from Making Noise.

My brother Mai was the sole orchestrator of Mother's funeral. Most of the guests were his business partners, sleek in black, hauling giant funeral wreaths, their cars blocking the cemetery gate. The brass band in eight identical white suits, looking like eight brothers. A dozen young men with flashing cameras, perhaps hired for the occasion, perhaps press. Another dozen young men walking around talking into radios, perhaps my brother's men, perhaps security guards from the local ward. An impressive plot of land, bounded by a thick wall on all four sides, a gravestone already erected, green granite, flanked by two hundred-year-old cypresses, and in the very middle of it all a censer as tall as a person. The glass coffin set in front of the censer, head to the east, feet to the west. The slanting rays of morning sun. The leisurely drift of clouds. The roses burning scarlet. *Amazing Grace*. Beyond the transparent glass, bathed in the pure, pure sunlight, my mother was an extraordinary vision haloed by the mystery of death.

My brother Mai and I stood facing the coffin, hands joined in prayer, faces grim and serious, heads slightly bowed. My brother in black áo dài and pants, I in black áo dài and pants, cut and color and material the same as my mother's, made by the same distinguished Sài Gòn tailor. I'd dressed early in the morning, my brother had taken one glance my way and reached for his phone. The makeup team with their tools materialized after only fifteen minutes, and my face was perfectly made up, powdered, and mascaraed, the way I never am in daily life. My brother cast a second glance my way and again reached for his phone. His men came back after only fifteen minutes with a black hat, in a black box, perhaps ready-made, perhaps bespoke, but fitting my head to a tee. Little Ngọc and Mike were also at the funeral, standing behind me and my brother, wearing smaller versions of our same attire. The distinguished Sài Gòn tailor, busy with the adults' clothes, must have instructed his assistant tailors so that the outfits for the whole family, both the living and the dead, would be of the same cut, same color, same material. Everything was so prompt and exact, you would think a whole team of assistants was waiting on my brother, ready to leap into action every time he reached for his phone.

When a considerable crowd had assembled, a camera crew of three slowly made their entrance. The burliest, also the youngest, was shouldering a large camera, its lens already open, emitting a constant stream of whirring sounds. The trio seemed to have just returned from a round of the cemetery for establishing shots, and now were ready for the main sequence. The shortest, also the oldest, looked the quintessential secretary, notebook and phone ever at the ready, looking up from time to time to exchange a few words with the third, obviously the leader, a tall and slender man with a Rhett Butler mustache, a fedora, and a pipe. The leader pointed at the coffin, and the young cameraman made a beeline for it, thrust his camera at my mother's face for minutes on end, then zoomed out for a full-body take, and then recorded what else I didn't know, since my head had to be fixed in a slight bow. Someone, who turned out to be the short secretary, took my hand and gestured at me to bow my head still lower so that he could whisper in my ear that it was my turn now, which meant the camera would next focus on my face. I was still trying to register this information when the secretary explained that I would have to remain unblinking for minutes on end, so that I wouldn't look asleep in the pictures, and that I would have to be especially careful because the black hat cast a shadow that extended to my upper lip. I nodded silently. It was my first time facing a camera, and a professional camera at that. I imagined that the short secretary had to make a round, or rounds, to whisper into the ears of anybody the camera deemed worthy to focus on. Of course, some would understand right away while others would be clueless, and he would have to repeat the directions, discreetly, given the general solemnity. He might have to repeat something a hundred times. A production secretary's job is no piece of cake, it turns out.

The sun was still gentle, the clouds still drifting, and the roses still exuding their head-spinning fragrance when *Amazing Grace* segued to *Requiem* and it was time to lower the coffin. After five minutes of music, my brother read a short eulogy along the lines of: our family is thankful for your presence and consideration, our beloved mother has led a simple life and would wish for a tranquil departure, grief is best kept in the heart, sorrows should not be overdone. His speech concluded in absolute silence on the part of the attendants (you could even hear the camera's whirring), perhaps partly due to his own heavy hints, but I enjoyed imagining that it was mainly because the guests were still in awe of the vision of my mother in her glass coffin). Without any instruction they had set their giant wreaths down in a corner and stood in neat rows, hands joined in prayer, faces grim and serious, heads slightly bowed, waiting for my brother's speech to conclude before they filed forward to admire mother one last time. Accompanied by the sound of the bugle, they each circled the gaping grave, paused a short while, threw a red rose and a handful of dirt into the grave, then turned to shake my brother's hand and mine, all in silence, heads still slightly bowed until they returned to their place. All gestures and expressions were done to perfection, suggesting plenty of opportunities to practice.

My brother shook everyone's hand and said thank you, and I also shook their hands and said thank you. My brother nodded, and I also nodded. My brother greeted someone as a Miss, and I did the same, or a Missus, and I followed suit, or a Mister, and I copied. In short, I parroted everything he did. His speech was the only time I was left on my own, looking from my mother in the glass coffin to the red roses, from the freshly dug earth to the fire ant hill by a cypress tree, all the while with my head still slightly bowed, face still grim and serious, hands still joined in prayer. The twenty minutes swiftly passed, and my black hat was still fast on my head. So it was not that hard after all, all it took was some concentration. Even little Ngọc and Mike could do it. When I watched the sixty-minute video and looked at the hundreds of photos afterward, I realized that the children, standing behind my brother and me, had parroted everything we did. The adults' gestures and expressions suggested plenty of opportunities to practice. The children's too were done to perfection, suggesting the same. As if all these people had gathered here today not to facilitate my mother's funeral, headed by my brother and me, but to play out a movie script, with the cast list as follows:

<table>
<tr><td>My brother Mai</td><td>as</td><td>the Elder Son,</td></tr>
<tr><td>Me</td><td>as</td><td>the Youngest Daughter,</td></tr>
<tr><td>Little Ngọc and Mike</td><td>as</td><td>the Grandchildren by Son and Daughter,</td></tr>
<tr><td>The funeral guests</td><td>as</td><td>the Funeral Guests,</td></tr>
<tr><td>A dozen young men with cameras</td><td>as</td><td>Cameramen-cum-Members of the Press,</td></tr>
<tr><td>A dozen young men with radios</td><td>as</td><td>Security Guards of the Local Ward-cum-Mai's Men,</td></tr>
</table>

and, obviously,

<table>
<tr><td>Our mother</td><td>as</td><td>the Deceased.</td></tr>
</table>

If my mother's funeral was a veritable work of cinematic art (some later went as far as saying it was on par with the best Hollywood productions), the highest praise must go to my brother Mai as the producer-*cum*-director. But the second praise, and not any lesser, I venture to say belongs to my mother. My mother and no one else, my mother who had chosen terrible pain so that her face would remain intact. Can you imagine if her face had been as wrecked as her body? Even the most expensive powder and mascara would have been in vain, the most seasoned makeup artists would have thrown in their towels, a wooden coffin would have been the only option, and a black brocade áo dài and red roses wouldn't have been called for. And in that case, no amount of divine intervention could have turned the guests into such gracious and devoted actors, because their setting the giant wreaths in the appropriate place without any instruction was itself a thing to be marveled at. The quiet, elegant, organized funeral would have been replaced by a noisy, rowdy, disorganized affair. Perhaps my mother's very presence, so exquisite and refined in her glass coffin, as commanding as that of a silver-screen veteran, had inspired the others to be the best actors they could be. The result being that everybody's gestures and expressions were as perfect as if they'd really had plenty of opportunities to practice. When I watched the sixty-minute DVD and looked at the hundreds of photos, I was surprised to see what talented actors they all were. I was surprised, too, to see myself in the pictures. As if a woman my age, with an appearance similar to mine, had been invited to take my place. That woman was perfectly made up, powdered, and mascaraed, the way I had never been. That woman was meticulously dressed up in a black áo dài, black pants, black hat, things I had never worn. That woman was capable of not blinking for minutes on end and displaying remarkable confidence before the camera. That woman was not me.

Suddenly I had a hunch that upon finding my mother's body, a wreck in a pool of blood, my brother had been no less impressed to find her face still intact. The dozen years building his career in Sài Gòn had given him ample opportunities to put various scripts into production (of which the elevator inauguration was on the modest side) and turned him into a shrewd director. He must have cast aside whatever emotion was in his heart and immediately sketched in his head a script worthy of the opportunity presented to him. How promptly and exactly he must have acted, to commission a large glass coffin and have it shipped all the way from Singapore to Sài Gòn. And all in seven days, surely a record.

2 Sài Gòn

An actual dead person playing the role of the deceased? Many directors had used a real policeman to play a policeman, a real girl of the street to play such a girl, a real MD to play a doctor, a real invalid to play a patient, a real Frenchman to play a Frenchman ... but a real dead person playing the deceased, that's something unheard of in the whole history of Hollywood. In certain, otherwise unremarkable, cinematic traditions, paradoxically, this feat is already achieved; case in point: the People's Republic of Korea. The total number of movies released in a year might be underwhelming, but since the death of Kim Il Sung, cinematic works revolving around the funeral of the Great Leader must number dozens. And they are not amateur flicks at all, but truly ambitious productions in which each participant performs to the best of their ability: fists thumping chests, knees giving way, faces distorted in mourning, hair disheveled ... A whole sea of people whose gestures and expressions are done to perfection, as if they've had plenty of opportunities to practice. And orchestras playing identical magnificent elegies, TV hosts making identical poignant speeches, secretaries of communist parties heaping on identical praise ... But the most vivid, most convincing role has to be the one performed by the deceased himself: the late Chairman Kim Il Sung, his head propped up on a high pillow, angled slightly to the left to hide the large swelling in the nape of his neck, a brilliant red flag draping his body, the body of a Chairman who at eighty-two was still blessed with rosy cheeks, taut skin and plump lips—the same face that's depicted on thirty-five thousand life-size statues dotting every corner of the People's Republic. On this day, the face is even more royal and awe-inspiring, haloed by the mystery of death.

In early July 1994, the Normal University of Hà Nội sent their condolences to the Normal University of Pyongyang and received, a week later, a ninety-minute video of the funeral of the Great Leader, which they screened two months later, at a National Day party on September 2, for the enjoyment of the whole staff and faculty. My mother, by then retired, was also invited. I imagine how from the front row, having downed a half glass of sour-and-sweet Thăng Long wine, my mother had watched the whole movie in a strangely pleasant lightheadedness. Surrounded by the sobbing of her former colleagues at the on-screen glass coffin plowing a sea of kerchief-clutching, thigh-striking, screaming people, my mother was the only one to grasp the extraordinariness of our comrades the Korean directors' innovation: *let the dead play the dead.* Perhaps that very moment had sowed the seed for my mother's dream of her own final performance. I remember how, for a whole month, my mother would gush to anyone who would listen about the one-in-a-million funeral of Chairman Kim, about the glass coffin that must have measured eight meters a side, glorious in the morning sun or shimmering amid tens of thousands of candles, and of course about the radiant visage of Chairman Kim. This dead face is so exquisite, no living person could dream of competing with it. The kind of exquisiteness that made twenty million of the living strike their thighs and scream their desire to die along with their beloved. "How extraordinary!" was my mother's favorite comment about it, a refrain that never lost any of its elation.

But her elation didn't always fall on receptive ears. Our country was then beginning to fall under the sweep of the global South Korean wave. People either knitted their brows at, or walked away from, my mother's enthusiasm for the North Korean funeral. Now that she was retired and wielded power no more, she could no longer thrust her finger at her listener's face, commanding them to sit still while the lady department head or vice secretary of the party committee was speechifying. But that didn't stop her. "How extraordinary!" kept bursting forth from her lips. For a whole month, she was a Chairman Kim superfan.

A veritable epiphany it was, but disappointment followed hot on its heels. After a month had passed my mother realized that an extraordinary dream is likely doomed to stay in the realm of dreams; in the whole People's Republic of Korea, Kim Il Sung alone was bestowed the honor of an actual dead person playing the deceased. That disappointment, or should we say ennui, descended on my mother the year she turned sixty, and for the next ten years it refused to leave. At sixty-nine, in 2004, for some reason she accepted my brother's invitation to come and inaugurate his elevator in Sài Gòn. It was only the second time she had visited the city. The first time, two decades earlier, was when she attended a conference of educators of the Southern provinces as a delegate from the Hà Nội Department of Education. That was in the early eighties, when the municipal guesthouse staff still thought napkins and tissues were interchangeable, so the sojourn didn't impress her much. But now, twenty years later, after a few days at my brother's house, a few times riding his home elevator, a few trips in his Mercedes, a few dinners at five-star hotels, and a few nights being charmed by American movies, my mother's impression of Sài Gòn had done an about-face and her dream of that final performance once again stirred in her heart, its North Korean spectacle now understandably replaced by Hollywood glamor. The elevator inauguration may have followed a modest script in my brother's book, but in my mother's, it was another life-altering epiphany. In the sixty-minute video, in the hundreds-strong photo albums, now and again I caught her eyes widening at a glittering necklace, her hands hesitating around knives and forks, her ears pricking up at female guests checking out one another's Louis Vuittons. And now and then I caught her humbled glances flickering down to her polyester áo dài from Hàng Đào Street with their embroidered dragons and phoenixes, her faux leather heels from the People's Republic of China with their heavy, stiff form, her turtle shell bangle from the Hà Nội Department Store with its varnish of old-person snobbery. It was true she played the part of the graceful and self-assured lady from the capital as best she could, but I could tell that turbulent thoughts swirled in her head while champagne foamed down stemmed glasses, while cameras flashed like summer stars, while four of Mai's men hauled a gigantic cake inside, while all around her people were wishing each other a few more billions of income, a few more title deeds to hold, a few more countries to visit.

3 Paris

I looked around the room one last time before turning off the light. The sparse room contained only the sets of plastic desks and chairs and the wall-mounted blackboard, likely also plastic, which I had come to know intimately. The last copy exercise remained on that blackboard, a short extract from a long poem that had flashed into my mind during my sprint here earlier from the Métro station in the heavy rain:

I still look for you through the pure
afternoon of Monday through the pure
lips inviting to stay through the pure
clouds over Hồ Tây through the pure
home where we play through the pure
day so fresh and gay through the pure
shoes of May so pure
for you

I closed the door and climbed the wooden stairs. Today's Vietnamese class had just concluded. My students were two elderly ladies who'd persisted since day one. All that was left of the original cohort. I hadn't wanted to assign them some exercise from the textbook today, but couldn't think of anything else but that long-forgotten poem. We had finished copying the passage, then idly sat and stared at one another. Then one of them suggested translating it into French. I agreed. So for the following half an hour, while my students each wrestled with their own doorstop of a Vietnamese–French dictionary, I let my mind wander back to the time I first discovered this poem, how I'd marveled at the utter simplicity of art. Those were my days as a newcomer to France, fresh off the boat, when a daily visit to the job center for overseas students meant a daily lesson in disappointment. Those were also the days I first tried my hand at writing short stories, when a nightly session typing away at the computer seemed a never-ending pursuit of that obscure object of desire.

A few doors down from the craft shop, there was a small awning over the sidewalk. I'd planned to run straight from the classroom to the Métro station, but the road was too slippery from the still-pouring rain. It was just past eight, but downtown Paris was already deserted. A man's voice drifted over from the apartment behind me: "Maria, I'm so sorry, from the bottom of my heart!" Then a short strain of music, then a woman's: "Octavio, you can't imagine how miserable I was during those days without you!" And then some more music, then the sound of what seemed the combined sobbing of a man and a woman. I glanced up at the building across the street; the windows on the first and second floors were flickering with reflected TV screens, in front of which silhouettes sat transfixed. On the very first day of class, one student had kindly advised me that the most popular movies are shown on Monday nights, so it was best I switch class to another day of the week. I shook my head no, and after two lessons he vanished without a trace. That night I looked up the TV schedules and was aghast: Mondays are when the television, already the dominant form of entertainment seven days a week, triumphs most definitively: it's when the broadcast companies bring out their biggest guns and the couch potatoes are simply spoiled for choice. After this discovery, I warmed significantly to the students who showed up on Monday nights. They at least were not easy prey to the almighty TV. But their ranks grew thinner each week.

At the beginning of September, I had to beg and plead so that Madame Wang would not cancel the Monday class altogether. I felt like if I let that happen, I too would have succumbed to the all-conquering TV.

My Vietnamese class came into being two years ago when Madame Wang realized that the basement under her craft shop was lying unused, the same shop where I worked as her assistant several days a week. Rent was murderously high, and the Asian knickknacks craze was beginning to wane. An invariably fair person, Madame Wang made it clear on the first day: shop or class, a day off meant a day's pay deducted, half a day off the same.

After my class had been running for a while, a poster advertising a Chinese class appeared on the shop window. Madame Wang had pushed aside a dozen adult-height mock-antique vases and managed to squeeze a blackboard and a row of plastic chairs inside the craft shop itself. Voilà, the aspiring Chinese speakers outnumbered the Vietnamese enthusiasts severalfold, and new students continued to pour in, even after all the ceramic stools for sale had been appropriated to serve as their seats. The entrepreneurial Madame Wang immediately announced more classes and recruited more students. The two Vietnamese classes a week were always taught beneath a roomful of Chinese babblers. It seemed like the shop was packed every night of the week. Sometimes the Chinese teacher and I ran into one another, but we only paused for the briefest exchange of greetings. Neither knew the other's name. The noise was still tolerable, except when the upstairs class learned to sing in Chinese, always the same song: *The East is red, the sun is rising, hu er hai ya.*

And now, walking on the rain-puddled pavement, I thought from now on I would never again be haunted on Monday by "The East is red." And never again would I have a chance to ask the meaning of that *hu er hai ya*. After half a year, the Monday students of both Chinese and Vietnamese classes had almost all been brought into the fold of TV worshippers. All that remained of the Vietnamese class was two elderly ladies. And the Chinese class today had been so empty that the teacher decided to send them all home from the start. Learning to sing had gone the way of the dodo.

4 Sài Gòn

Perhaps because he wanted a no less Hollywoodian denouement for his script, when the grave had just been filled in and covered with roses, my brother Mai announced that he would love to invite everyone present to a *simple meal with the family*. They arrived at the top floor of a five-star hotel overlooking the Bạch Đằng Quay to find a buffet waiting, fifty dishes in all, vegetarian choices available, wine and champagne included.

They quickly arranged themselves into groups, which for some reason formed along age lines. The elderly, a look of awe still lingering on their faces, glanced at one another in silence. The middle-aged talked in low voices for a few minutes, then one couple climbed up and leaned against the railing with outstretched arms, necks craning towards the Sài Gòn river, hair fluttering in the wind in an impression of the *Titanic* scene. Hollywood seemed still to have them under its spell. A hotel staff member ran out in panic, perhaps taking them for some wannabe Korean lovers with a suicide pact. The youngsters kept shrieking with laughter. A handsome boy took off his cravat and threw it into the river. A few others followed suit. One even threw his socks. In a daze I thought, how fortunate the cameras had remained fixed at the graveyard's gate right until the final moments, so that the amateur actors remained disciplined when climbing onto their bikes, revving their engines in unison without my brother having to ask for the ward police to step in. With the ward police invading the script, how much less Hollywoodian would it have become?

My brother Mai poured an endless stream of champagne, for others and then for himself, and sometimes even for me. The atmosphere was a mix of solemnity and rowdiness. The handsome boy sans cravat suggested some dance music. My brother asked for more champagne, poured the boy a full glass, led him to the buffet table, advising he eat something. But the boy acted as if he was confused, and the moment my brother turned his back the boy ran to his pack, then there was a shattering sound. The middle-aged couple on the railing were now kneeling on the floor, back to back, heads tilted upward, hair still fluttering in the wind, rom-com style, their love of acting apparently still unexhausted.

When the evening was well underway, a woman in a black miniskirt approached us; hand on my brother's shoulder, she looked at me and said, "Why don't you introduce us to your française sister who came home to play with us?" I wanted to correct her that Mike and I taking a six a.m. bus to Roissy last week to catch the earliest flight to Sài Gòn was not in order to *play* but to attend my mother's funeral. But then I thought better of it. Deep in my heart, I felt that I, like all the others, was there only in order to *act*, and acting is after all a kind of playing, this is something that can be agreed upon in both the English and French languages.

Taking the woman's hand, my brother put it on the table and put a glass of champagne in it before turning to me: "This is Miss Diễm Lan, queen of the Sài Gòn art scene." I nodded, and just at that moment caught sight of the whitest stockings below the miniskirt hem, and at the end of those whitest stockings the whitest pair of heels. Noticing my glance, Miss Diễm Lan leaned back against Mai, her hand on the table also sporting the whitest nails with a few specks of glitter, the very picture of beauty and the beastillionaire. I took a sip of champagne, which was probably enough to knock me out, for the top floor darkened around me, the boys one by one disappeared, Miss Diễm Lan was now tottering on her plastered legs, her ten fingers ten merry glowworms dancing around, now nudging Mai's chest, now going into hiding under the tables.

My brother reached for his phone. A moment later two of his men ran to us and helped me into the elevator, to the ground floor, to the SUV already waiting in front of the hotel with his chauffeur behind the wheel. Running after me was the housekeeper, also drunk on champagne, longing for home and a sobering bitter gourd drink. Bringing up the rear was Mike, who climbed onto the seat on his own, unbothered by champagne but wondering aloud what *bitter god* was and if he could have a bite. No one answered him. Perhaps no one understood what he said.

Dazzling asphalt. Dazzling sun. Obliterating white leaves. I closed my eyes, my head drumming. The car kept swerving close to the curb, and the chauffeur grumbled: "*Tese* fucking *Soutern* bastards don't know how to drive." Every single person in my brother's employ was from the North, including the housekeeper, just shy of sixty, a former apparatchik from the Women's Affairs Committee of the Hải Dương Ceramic Factory who'd drifted southward to clean his house and wash his dishes. Every swerve of the car made her press both hands to her chest and whine to be let off to catch a bike taxi. The chauffeur said nothing, but his sunglasses scowled, every inch a tough guy from Hải Phòng.

The hum of the air conditioner could be heard in the silence. Suddenly Mike piped up to ask me to let him sleep in my room tonight, he was "scared" of sleeping alone. I looked at the housekeeper, then at the chauffeur, who remained a scowling pair of sunglasses. *Scared* seemed a word the adults had been avoiding since my mother's demise. The day Mike and I arrived, my brother had told the housekeeper to prepare two separate rooms, en suite, separated by a large, absolute hallway. Maybe that was why Mike was scared. I didn't respond. Neither did the housekeeper. The chauffeur reached out and turned on the car stereo. Out came the voice of Quynh Anh: *One day I'll touch your soil /*

One day I'll finally know your soul / One day I'll come to you / To say hello … Vietnam.

The car swerved and swerved. Perhaps the chauffeur had fallen asleep, but it was hard to say with his sunglasses and lack of snoring. People from the port city are legendary for their special skills. Fortunately at this hour the hardworking traffic cops would be enjoying a nap. And Sài Gòn streets are mostly straight, with few trees and narrow sidewalks. I got to know Sài Gòn at thirty thanks to my mother's funeral. My brother had called me on my cell phone and said, "A return ticket from Paris to Sài Gòn. I'll reimburse the cost." I said nothing. He continued, "If both of you come, I'll pay for you both." Then he hung up, and I spent the night wondering what else he knew about me besides Mike's existence.

As the swan-white exterior of the Rex Hotel came into view across the boulevard, the car began circling Nguyễn Huệ roundabout. It was three o'clock and the temperature was thirty-nine degrees, clouds were absent, the humidity was eighty-three percent, the air was still. Continuing down Lê Thánh Tôn Street, we finally came to the black gate of my brother's place. I had to tickle Mike's neck before he opened his eyes and got out, yawning and asking for his bitter god drink. No one answered. Presumably no one understood this time either.

Dazzling sun. Obliterating white leaves. Mike stood alone in the yard. His hair was blond. His eyes were blue. When he was an infant, Parisians would come up to us in the Jardin du Luxembourg and asked me if I was his nanny. Three days ago, Saigonese people kept approaching me in Đầm Sen Park and asked me if I was his parents' maid. Mike was five when he showed up at the immigration booth at Tân Sơn Nhất Airport. No nationality, no passport, all he had was a three-by-four photograph glued to the second to last page of mine. No father's name, no father's family name, on his birth certificate "father" was blank, "mother" was me, his family name was mine, his name was Mike, pronounced "Mick" as the French said or "mai" in the Vietlish way. I don't know how a French-language teacher from the Normal University of Hà Nội would call him, since my mother had never met him.

My brother, who picked us up at the airport, called him Michael, and immediately all his men called him Michael Jackson; as she fried some nem, the housekeeper said she would now serve little Nickson some nem so that little Nickson would not bomb the North back to the stone age, so that the North can finish building their socialism. Mike asked what socialism was, and if he could have a bite. Cue general laughter. Ngọc wanted to take the day off to go to Đầm Sen and watch Hong Kong movies with her little cousin. The girl was the only one to pronounce his name right, but he was the only one to pronounce hers wrong. Gock, nock. Another round of laughter.

In the morning my brother brought an envelope full of dollars to the international hospital to pay for my mother's funeral service, then took the whole family to some hotel for breakfast, and then the whole family dropped Ngọc off at the Vietnam-Australia International School. The housekeeper was taken along for the meal, but she never dared say what she wanted for herself and insisted on finishing the children's leftovers. The chauffeur always stayed in the car, stretched out on the back seat and listening to "Bonjour Vietnam," always nodding off after a few bars, and when we wanted to bring him something to eat he always claimed to have already eaten at home. My brother shook his head. He couldn't be expected to provide breakfast for all those builders and office workers.

5 Sài Gòn

It was the morning after my mother's funeral and my brother Mai said, let me treat you all to fine Chinese dining. He first called the Vietnam-Australia International School to ask for another day off for Ngọc, who was still mourning her grandmother. He would also, he promised, gift the school board with a sixty-minute DVD of the funeral, bilingual. The children begged to go in yesterday's mourning clothes, which they thought made them look like Hong Kong movie stars.

The car stopped in front of a weathered three-story restaurant, whose red sign was mostly hidden behind a large old tree, the black lines of its Chinese name already flaking off. The car door opened to let in a head-spinning smell of food, and my brother and I got out. At the end of the street I glimpsed a sign that let me know we were on Hải Thượng Lãn Ông Street, the famous Chợ Lớn hub of Chinese medicine. A long-haired youth ran out, said to my brother nǐ hǎo, shook the chauffeur's hand, gestured that he should park on the sidewalk, then turned his smiling face to me and said, "Hà Nội ah?" I don't remember if I nodded yes or no, but I remember that he winked at my brother and spewed forth a torrent of Chinese. Blushing, my brother shook his head.

The car was finally parked with the front half on the sidewalk and the back on the street, a gurgling stream of gutter water passing beneath it, and next to it an old gentleman in a fedora sitting on a stool, hawking mysterious things in two big black barrels and a pot noisily boiling on a coal stove. The scowling chauffeur went to open the rear door. The housekeeper was the first to fly out, and added some nice white vomit to the gutter. The children were next. At the sight of Mike, the long-haired youth visibly paled, glanced over to my brother, who forged ahead, at me, who looked away, and finally at the housekeeper, who gave him a withering side-eye. Mike held Ngọc's hand and waltzed in nonchalantly. A week in Sài Gòn had already taught him a few things.

Beyond the narrow façade the path went deep inside, winding and snaking ever more in the dim light, giving off the impression of a labyrinth. In the belly of that labyrinth I imagined hundreds of people merrily cooking, eating, drinking, and tasting things for which there is no word in Vietnamese, all oblivious to the elevator and its accident. It is said that for the Chinese in Vietnam, comfort is ephemeral and cuisine is life. My brother held Ngọc's hand and mine, I held Mike's, Mike held the housekeeper's. A five-person family chain clinging to one another. It was difficult enough on the flat ground, but a real challenge climbing the stairs. We stumbled and bumbled and barely avoided falling down. Passing a series of drafty, smoke-stained, low-ceilinged rooms, we finally stepped inside a space with a high ceiling and white walls and curtains on the windows. Apparently the day before our mother's funeral, my ever-busy brother had found time to reach for his phone and have his men book a *special* room.

We sat down on five chairs whose shell-inlaid backs depicted a sparrow couple bringing home their find. The children turned to each other and made chirping sounds. The housekeeper, pale as death, had already made a few dashes for the toilet outside and now sat clutching at her chest, her throat incessantly jerking. The hungry children began to whine. The waiter brought in a wooden tray, and in each of the five ceramic bowls on it there was a pinkish fowl with its eyes shut, in a viscous liquid.

Mike looked at me. I looked at Ngọc. Ngọc looked at Mai. My brother smiled. The waiter too: "Please eat the blood swiftlets while they're hot."

The children burst out crying, saying they wouldn't eat the sparrows, then jumped from their chairs and insisted on going home. The waiter, still smiling, pointed at Mike and said, "Blood swiftlets, good for albinos."

Mike didn't react to the remark, presumably not understanding either *blood swiftlets* or *albinos,* but Ngọc grabbed a chopstick and threatened to put the waiter's eyes out. Her command of Sino-Vietnamese was really quite good, certainly not thanks to the international school but more likely to the Chinese movie industry. The housekeeper and I immediately rushed to restrain her. The waiter put the tray on the table and ran out, hands over his eyes.

The crying children still insisted on going home. Mai had to take matters into his own hands. He ordered stir-fried phở for Ngọc and fried nem for Mike. The restaurant would have to send someone off on his bike with a lunch box to procure those things. In Chợ Lớn you can only buy Chinese food. The long-haired youth volunteered. Fifteen minutes later, when the food was on the table, he caressed Mike's hair and said the boy was as handsome as Brad Pitt, perhaps in way of making amends.

Ngọc, still seething throughout the wait, had her chopstick ready to put out the waiter's eyes the moment he stepped inside, but after half a starving hour the smell of the stir-fried phở captured all her attention. The waiter took the opportunity to ask if the family wanted to listen to traditional operetta, enjoying blood swiftlets to the songs of traditional operetta is how the connoisseurs do it. Mike asked what *traditional omelleta* was, and if he could have a bite. Mai and I laughed.

The housekeeper raised her bowl to take a sip, then sighed, "Now I can die already." She had been fasting since yesterday in anticipation of the blood swiftlets, hence her carsickness. I tried a spoonful, somewhat sweet and somewhat tangy, but nothing more remarkable than steamed stuffed pigeons in Cấm Chỉ Alley. I tasted it once a long time ago in Hà Nội, before I left for France.

My brother and the housekeeper ended up with two bowls

each, as the children refused to touch theirs. On the way home Mai kept silent, but smiled from time to time. This morning he didn't wear his light gray suit but jeans and a striped polo with the crocodile logo. He was forty-five and a picture of health. He had gone through two divorces and now held an important position in the Sài Gòn real estate scene. Fifteen years ago, he was tall and rail thin, riding a high Russian bicycle, with no wife on the horizon and a precarious contract teaching math and physics at Cần Thơ University. In those fifteen years my brother and I hadn't once talked. I couldn't help but reconsider the question that had cost me a sleepless night: what else did he know about me, besides Mike's existence?

It was the morning after my mother's funeral.

6 Paris

A seven-story building, a gray gate, a prison's level of security. My watch read fifteen hundred. It was already an hour since Paul Polotsky disappeared behind the gray gates. I didn't know which apartment he was visiting, whom he was seeing, or how long he would stay. All I could do was to follow my target.

Today Paul Polotsky hadn't followed his usual route to his reading bench in the park. After class, from the campus gate, he suddenly headed to the Métro station at a surprising speed. I hurried after him. With every step my target seemed even more energetic, while I had to thread my way through a host of towering northern European tourists who stopped every few minutes to aim their cameras. My heart drumming, it was like this was an entirely different person I was dealing with. Polotsky seemed to have the whole course laid out in his mind. He went swiftly down to the Métro, switched at every few stops, and passed down long, forking corridors without pausing to consult a map. I had to run most of the way to breathlessly keep up with him. At the end of Line 4, he got out the moment the train stopped and glided into a small corridor that led to another, even smaller, emerging onto the street in under a minute, and then walked intently, even faster, as if his destination was imminent.

So I was surprised when he suddenly slowed down as the road led up onto an iron bridge. Not a soul in sight. Cold sweat dampened my back in the thirty-nine-degree heat. If Polotsky only turned his head, he would discover his stalker right at his heels. Fortunately, he only dropped his speed and gazed into the distance, where tall buildings stood cracked in the summer heat. Down below, the multilane highway was busy. A giant truck bearing the logo of a Chinese supermarket chain swerved and pulled to the curb. Near the far end of the bridge, Polotsky stopped and put his briefcase and overcoat on the railing. I was expecting a long wait, but my target suddenly stooped and took out a pair of sunglasses to replace his large reading glasses, smoothed his hair, then continued on his way. That night at home, I would check the map and discover that the iron bridge was what separates Paris and the small town of Montrouge. That was the first time I set foot in the southern banlieue.

My next hour flew by, thanks to the door lady. She had arrived in France with her parents fifty years ago, and now, after trying in vain to grab hold of her youngest daughter, she poured her sorrow upon me as I paced outside the gates waiting for Polotsky. She told me in her Thanh Hóa accent how the pet name they gave the girl, *our darling the Princess of Annam,* had planted in the kid's mind delusions of grandeur. Little did the daughter know that her fine dresses, her ballet lessons, her Vietnamese dulcimer lessons were paid for by her mother's working hours of janitoring, and after-work hours of bathing and manicuring a dozen elderly tenants, and her father's days of stir-frying noodles at his main restaurant, nights of frying at his side diner, and weekends of frying at home so that supermarket customers could get their noodles in plastic boxes. Little did she understand why the money they had borrowed from banks and acquaintances went not into a decent apartment, but a convertible Mercedes to take her to school and elsewhere. Each day she longed for the moment she could go out, leaving their narrow room with too faint sunlight and too thick a smell of stir-fried noodles, put on her white silk dress trimmed with pearls and be transformed, sitting in the back seat of the Mercedes, into a princess. At school, at fashion boutiques, at cram school, everybody was mesmerized by her, mistaking her parents for her au pair and chauffeur. Her delusions had grown more entrenched as the years went by, until she was convinced that she had been kidnapped from the palace as an infant by none other than these impostor parents. Earlier this year she had insisted that the three of them take a DNA test.

"Ridiculous, right?"

I forgot to nod until the door lady mildly slapped my shoulder. I had drunk in every word of that outlandish story, but the moment she asked me the question the gray gates flew open and a gaggle of retired apparatchiks flowed out, some carrying duffel bags, some dragging along suitcases. Two silver minibuses instantly materialized. Happy as larks, the whole delegation got on them, having shaken hands and patted backs and promised to meet again to their hearts' content. I had to look hard to detect any sign of Polotsky, and only nodded at the door lady when the two silver minibuses had darted away, leaving two puffy clouds of silver smoke. My head nodded but my mind was wondering if perhaps, in the last few confusing minutes, my target had left the building and was now immersed in counting his paces along some endless station corridor. The door lady however paid no heed to the apparatchiks or the minibuses; she had picked up her laments about the youngest daughter who could now never be seen at school nor at home. The girl's reasoning was: her parents had refused a DNA test because they feared they would be found out.

"Ridiculous, right?"

This time I was frozen mid-nod: the gray gates flew open again, five or six children ran out, and in their wake, finally, loomed the droopy figure of Polotsky, the sunglasses still occupying his nose. Nothing could be seen of his usual listlessness, or the energy of a few hours ago; my target was now holding his briefcase in one hand, his other arm draped around the shoulders of a woman no less droopy, whose dress came down to her heels and whose face was virtually invisible under a wide-brimmed mahogany-colored hat. This very hat helped me to locate them ten minutes later, when they had passed down the street and merged into a crowd waiting for the lights. During those exasperating ten minutes, every time I was about to make a dash for it the door lady would hold me back with a *Ridiculous, right?* Luckily for me, the *Princess of Annam* herself abruptly appeared. I lowered my head and drove my legs as fast as I could past the girl's pallid face, and moments later heard shouts behind me. Presumably, her royal highness had again escaped the door lady's paws.

Shops lined both sides of the street in the town center. Nearby rose a church spire as tiny as a toy. It was the most frantic time of the sales season, and the streets dazzled with legs and smells. Polotsky was no longer walking beside the woman but immediately behind. The two droopy figures were walking and chatting as if they were the only ones around. But I didn't catch a word, with the distance being too far and the woman's voice too low, barely more than a whisper, so that Polotsky himself had to keep dipping his ear toward her wide-brimmed hat. His sunglasses nodded as incessantly as his lips moved, both inaudible. I didn't know if the woman herself caught a word. Then I imagined maybe she was deaf, seeing how she didn't nod or shake her head. Finally, to distract myself from my aching legs, I imagined a romance à la Stendhal. The long dress, the wide-brimmed hat, the church spire, the sunglasses, the beau and the beauty . . . it took my mind off my legs for a few minutes.

Whether behind or to the left of them, I maintained a strict distance of one meter and the guise of an ardent window-shopper. But after fifteen minutes of this my patience ran out and I decided to draw nearer, once even stopping right beside my targets now pausing in front of a hat shop. I twisted my neck to see her face in a mirror inside the window, and got an eyeful of reflected sun, but it was worth it to be able to eavesdrop on their conversation:

"Every time I pass this shop I look at this hat. Year after year, it seems to lie there waiting for me on the shelf. I wonder how it's possible that no one has taken possession of such a beautiful hat."

"Why didn't you ever tell me that you're fond of this hat? What other things are you keeping hidden from me?"

"It is too late now, you see. The hat no longer suits me at my age. And as for the other things, you can no longer do anything about them."

I was disappointed by those hollow words, not to mention his panting right next to me. The woman seemed to have more to say but walked away to peek in another shop. Polotsky followed her, his head lowered, his breathing still labored. I resumed my one-meter distance. It was not easy to keep near them anyway: anyone who threatened to come between them was thrust away by the droopy Polotsky. This man's strength seemed to be something to reckon with.

The street grew more and more crowded. I did a constant dance between sweat-covered bodies and bursting plastic bags. At an artificial flower shop, the woman suddenly turned back. If it weren't for the wide-brimmed hat I would have had her whole face in my sight. Another conversation began, her voice now less hushed:

"Do you remember the first flowers you gave me?"

"Of course. I knew at first sight that you are a lilac girl."

"You have never given me red roses."

"Indeed, I know you don't like them."

I sighed. What if my targets' talk never departed from these inanities? But just as I began to lament a wasted evening, Polotsky stepped up to squeeze the woman's shoulders, she turned sharply away, moved through the crowd and walked out into the road. A taxi somehow materialized. The rear door opened, she bolted in, she slammed the door, the car sped away.

It was over in a flash. Stunned, I could do nothing but stare. When my senses returned, I turned to the side to see Polotsky looking equally dazed. A young couple were rushing toward us, arms laden with bags upon bags, watching the vanishing exhaust smoke and crying out in frustration. It turned out they'd called a taxi a good half hour ago, and secured this one after a dozen calls only to see it swiped by the woman in the wide-brimmed hat when they were still stepping out of the shop.

Another ten minutes had passed but Polotsky hadn't shaken off his daze. He stood there, still, in the middle of the pavement, facing the direction the taxi had driven away, his dark sunglasses growing darker on his white face under his white hair. I was a few steps away from him, afraid that my target might collapse any minute, either because of an acute heart attack or the marching crowd all around, the sweat-covered bodies hugging bursting plastic bags. I was still debating whether to run to support him, or to wait and see what would happen if he kept standing there, not unlike a few days ago at that public park, when a tropical rain suddenly came down on Paris.

My parched throat was about to drive me into the nearest convenience store for some bottled water when Polotsky was jolted back to consciousness, shivered, rearranged his coat, fixed his glasses, smoothed his hair, and numbly started walking. I had to silence my now raging thirst and go with him back the way we had come, to the iron bridge, which was now oven-hot and disheveled.

Down below on the highway, the threads of traffic were still tightly woven. The giant Chinese supermarket truck had been replaced by a mighty triple convoy from a Bulgarian food company. Just as I'd feared, Polotsky didn't go straight to the Métro station, but listlessly stepped onto the bridge, listlessly stopped at the same spot as earlier, placed his overcoat and briefcase on the railing and then listlessly gazed into the distance, where there was nothing to see but a few cracked tall buildings.

We were once again the only ones on the bridge. If he grabbed me and threw me down onto the highway, Mike would be taken to the police station to wait for me there tonight. The scenario was not that improbable: he was much stronger than I'd imagined, while I, on the contrary, was much weaker.

To distract myself from my fear, I pictured an iced bottle of lemonade. Then to distract myself from that iced vision, I picked up the imagined romance where I had left off: time and again, Polotsky had crossed this bridge to visit the woman in the mahogany-colored hat, and each time he had stopped at this spot. There had once been a time when those buildings were much newer, or even freshly built, not yet inhabited. There would have been less traffic on the highway, and no Chinese supermarket trucks filling the lanes. The door lady would have been a new bride, spending her days dreaming pleasant dreams about a daughter as lovely and elegant as the *Princess of Annam*, whom she had glimpsed just once in *Paris Match*. Polotsky himself wouldn't have been touched by old age, still looking out of those limpid eyes. The woman would have been so youthful in a narrow-brimmed hat and a miniskirt showing off her knees. In summer evenings even hotter than this. In winter evenings sad and wilting, sometimes with snow. In autumn evenings with a smattering of rain and yellow leaves floating on the river. The lilacs could well have been the color lilac.

And my mother? Where was her place in this romance? I sighed to myself as I followed Polotsky down from the iron bridge.

In the Métro, in an immense corridor at Montparnasse station, I stopped in front of a vending machine for an chilled bottle of lemonade, and he vanished.

7 Sài Gòn

The Sài Gòn sun had been shining since six. At noon there was a sudden rain shower. The bike taxi driver flicked away his half-smoked cigarette, nodded and announced a gentle enough price. It was five minutes after I had dialed the number provided by the housekeeper. The phone had been picked up before the first ring ceased. I suggested meeting at his place, and he agreed. I suggested meeting right then, and he agreed. It all happened so fast I felt dizzy.

From a dark corner of his ground-floor living room, Mr. Linh watched me in silence, in total contrast with his willingness over the phone. He had been silent, in fact, from the very moment I walked in. When the bike taxi driver let me off, I had found the gate already open. It took me a minute to register my host. He was sitting in a dark corner and was dressed in black. I didn't know where to put myself. I just hovered awkwardly in the middle of the room.

Finally, figuring I wouldn't ever get invited to do so, I sat down on the sofa facing my host, which was like facing a black bronze statue. The pedestal fan behind me produced gusts of baking air. Not a picture on the wall, not a photo frame or even a stain that could help distract me from his gaze. I had to keep assuring myself that I was in his line of sight only by accident, and that there is no need to take account of the gaze of a statue.

He wouldn't be the one to break the silence, that was my disappointed conclusion. Finally, I gathered the courage to say that if I might venture a guess, he and my mother had known each other for a long time, and not from Sài Gòn. The first part, about theirs being a long-standing acquaintance, I was fairly sure of, because he had told the housekeeper that he was my mother's "old friend," but the second part, about not being from Sài Gòn, was purely intuitive. That intuition had stuck with me from the moment I first heard his voice on the phone, a Hanoian voice of the kind that could now rarely be heard, and only in Sài Gòn or Paris, a Hanoian voice that belongs to someone who has been away from Hà Nội for at least half a century.

Not a footstep in the house. Not a sound of any motor out in the alley. In the whizzing drone of the fan, Mr. Linh suddenly said:

"Fifty years ago."

The photo of Polotsky stirred in my pocket. It, too, had been taken fifty years ago. A harsh sound came from above. Something made of glass dropped onto a floor of marble. Mr. Linh's eyes were still fixed on me. I bowed my head slightly, to avoid looking into those eyes, to be able to listen to his incredible story:

"We met fifty years ago, in Hỏa Lò, on the very day she was captured. I was not a comrade. I was an interpreter. I was born in the same year as her. Flipping through her file, I was startled to see how she became a liaison girl for the Việt Minh on the same day I began my life under the payroll of the French government. During the years when her higher-ups were sending her to this or that place on this or that mission, mine were doing the same to me. We nearly crossed paths in numerous places. But fate wanted us to meet not by the verdant Sword Lake, in the ancient Trấn Quốc Pagoda, or at any of the other romantic sites for which Hà Nội is famous, but in the very Maison Central of Hỏa Lò. To a nineteen year old, to find yourself in a prison, and in Hỏa Lò of all places, means misfortune, whatever the reason. At the sight of her, tied at the crooks of her arms behind her back and with one side of her face swollen, I ran to the toilet and vomited my guts out. It was her first time being interrogated, and it was my first time having to go home from a job. Of course the higher-ups didn't want business to be delayed, they found a new interpreter immediately, one with more experience and better physical strength. I lay sleepless that whole night. And back at my desk the following morning I couldn't focus on my work. At noon, I gave up and went to Hỏa Lò, on the excuse of having left my logbook there. There were three people in the room. The senior interpreter, whom I had known for a long time, the Deuxième Bureau agent I had met the day before, and the third—a young white man, but after all these years I have forgotten what he looked like. The agent said he was the nephew of a higher-up in the Bureau, his name was Paul and his family name was something as tongue-twisting as the first name was simple, the moment it went in my ear it went out the other."

Silence enveloped the room once more. After that sound of glass smashing, the floor upstairs had long since returned to its quiet. The ever so patient fan produced gust after gust of hot air. I looked at Mr. Linh. The black bronze statue had returned to its place. I wondered why, when talking about my mother, Mr. Linh didn't ever use her name, though he knew it from the intelligence agency file. Neither did he use the romanticizing *nàng*, as Nhất Linh or Khái Hưng or any author from Tự lực văn đoàn might have done, in the novels that had colored the halcyon days of their generation. Neither did he call her the youthful *cô ấy*, though she was but nineteen years old at the time. He only ever used the one word, full of respect: *bà*.

Another minutes-long silence ensued before Mr. Linh continued his story, that while waiting for my mother in the interrogation room, he talked to Paul and was surprised to learn that they were the same age. The thought struck him that the three of them, all born in the same year, were destined for such different fates. Paul was as dewy-eyed as Linh and my mother were hardened. The day my mother became a liaison girl for the Việt Minh and Linh began life as an employee of the French military, Paul had enrolled in a liberal arts university. At the end of his sophomore year, he rewarded himself with an adventure to Indochina, the land he'd learned about in books—and books only—and Hà Nội was his first stop. While the Vietnamese avoided Hỏa Lò like the plague it was, Paul solicited his Deuxième Bureau uncle to fix him a visit to the notorious place, to bless his adventure with a real sense of adventure. At nineteen, Paul had already left one romance behind. At nineteen, Linh lost sleep over a woman for the first time. When out in the corridor the sound of footsteps drew near, the senior interpreter and the agent looked at him in derision. My mother was let in the moment he had to walk out. They were face to face for that one moment. On that threshold. His heart skipped a beat. My mother's arms were still tied behind her back, but the bruise on her face was gone. For the next fifty years, he confessed, he never encountered anyone as beautiful as my mother, whose classic Hanoian beauty was imbued with a hint of something he couldn't quite put his finger on. At nineteen, a person is still nebulous. At nineteen, a woman still hasn't bloomed into her full radiance, and a man is still in search of himself. Mr. Linh didn't know if he had loved my mother. He had never believed in love at first sight. But then again, he had never been so obsessed. *A fatal obsession.* As a teenager he had always smirked at this phrase so beloved by novelists. Purple prose making mountains out of molehills, he had always assumed.

In the afternoon, Linh sought to get into Hỏa Lò again. It was easy and yet, at the same time, highly problematic. The easiness came from his being employed by the French administration. The problem was that an employee loitering without reason in the political prisoners' ward ran the risk of making the agency's blacklist himself. He had no good excuse for being present in the interrogation room and he didn't even know if my mother would be in that day. He spent the afternoon in the guards' station, gazing over at the women prisoners' building. The February air was bitingly cold. He was standing in the attic, which gave little shelter due to some imminent renovation. He picked the place for that reason, because no guard would ever choose to go there of their own volition and risk being exposed to the wind. And what a wind it was, which coupled with that humidity chilled you to the bone. Later, when he had moved to Sài Gòn, whenever Mr. Linh thought of Hà Nội in winter it was that afternoon he would think of. A chill to the bone. A bite into your flesh.

After he had been there for around an hour the guard led a group of female prisoners to the bathhouse. Dozens of them, young and old, huddled together in groups, perhaps against the cold. In those baggy gray uniforms, with their unkempt hair over their faces, it was hard to tell one from the other. And they kept their faces turned to the ground as they walked. You wouldn't know it until you watched from that vantage point, Mr. Linh said: the law didn't demand it, but the guards never let prisoners raise their faces. He comforted himself with the thought he would recognize my mother in any crowd. But he waited and waited. Several such groups had gone by, but my mother wasn't in any of them. The temperature continued to drop, And the wind grew stronger. At five, when it became too dark to see anything, he left. It was either that or freeze to death. Both were unbearable. The saying goes, *a seventeen year old can break a buffalo's horn,* but in his experience a nineteen year old can't bear much, neither physically nor mentally, especially when already suffering from a *fatal obsession.*

Another sleepless night. Sedatives were unheard of back then. The next morning, looking into the shaving mirror, he promised himself that this would be the last time he returned to the prison. He had a family to support. He'd found a job right after getting his *baccalauréat,* because his father had passed away and he needed to support his siblings through their education. He dropped by the office to ask for one final day of leave. He dared not offer a reason, just bowed his head and walked away, his heart torn between submission and grimness.

The light was on in the interrogation room. And as bizarre fate would have it, Linh found himself in the company of the three figures from the morning before. Again the senior interpreter and the agent looked at him with derision. Only Paul was merry. He jokingly asked why Linh still hadn't found his logbook. Linh registered the joke but his eyes were on the door. He didn't hear whatever else Paul droned on about, his ears were trying to catch any coming footsteps. At nine sharp, the agent stood up and said they had a tight schedule today, apart from *that cute Vietmin* there were nearly ten other political prisoners due to be interrogated as a matter of urgency, the Điện Biên situation was now critical. Linh knew immediately who *that cute Vietmin* referred to. He also knew that my mother was about to be led in, and he had to find a way to remain in the room.

He tried to strike up a conversation with Paul, who seemed equally eager to talk, and similarly reluctant to leave. Then the sound of footsteps could be heard out in the corridor. Linh's heart skipped a beat. To hide his nervousness, he tried to keep his eyes wide open and fixed on Paul's face. It appeared to him that Paul was also nervous and trying to keep his own eyes wide open and fixed on Linh's face. But Linh had no time to find out why. He stood up and walked to the door. And the scene from the day before was repeated: my mother was led in the moment Linh had to step out. They were face to face for just that one moment. On the threshold. My mother raised her hand to her temple to tidy a strand of hair. Her lips curved ever so slightly. That curve of the lips forced him to place his hand on the wall to steady himself. That was the last time he saw my mother. The next day, at the office, he was told that she had been released. But he kept the promise he made to himself.

After the battle of Điện Biên and the Genève Conference, as an employee of the French, Linh got permission to bring his family to France. But his mother wouldn't hear of leaving Vietnam. It was only in August 1954, when the last flights out were already full, that the family found a way to Hải Phòng and got on some gaping-mouthed landing craft as part of the last wave of the exodus south. During those indelible two weeks of endless, uncertain voyaging, while others were nostalgic for Hà Nội or hopeful about Sài Gòn, Linh's every waking moment was consumed by the image of my mother's face. The indecipherable curve of her lips. Again he was flushed, again he had to steady himself against something. There was a fire in his stomach. He slumbered on in a terrible fever, a fever so bad he was certain that death was polishing a scythe with his name on it, but when the ship was about to dock at Sài Gòn he felt an impossible lightness. His body was no longer feverish but ice-cold. In that instant he understood that his *fatal obsession* was cured, his illness was gone, but from then on he would become another person. At high noon the summer sky and the river suddenly turned red, a violent red like none he had ever seen. Thunder and lightning soon followed. Then rain, a true tropical rain. A tropical rain baptized him as a Saigoneer.

With each hot salty drop beating on his skin, which was paper-thin after days looking death in the face, he told himself that nearly two thousand kilometers lay between them now. The seventeenth parallel had sliced the country in half. The media was excited about the general election that was to happen in two years. But Linh knew that day would never come.

I stood up, the black-and-white photo again stirring in my pocket. I felt I ought to go, because Mr. Linh's manner became very cold after finishing his story, he kept sniffing and looking at his wristwatch. He seemed not so much relieved at having freed himself from his burden as regretful for having disclosed it. I looked out the door. The iron gates had remained open throughout the talk.

I walked out of the alley to find a bike taxi. The rain had long since ceased. Alleys are the most distinguishing urban feature of Sài Gòn, big alleys begetting smaller ones. I wasn't sure if I was walking out of the right alley, if I was heading to the small bridge that the bike taxi driver had called cầu Bông, at the crossroads near the end of which there were two roasted-duck shops where customers were still queuing up at one p.m. Walking under a sun that was none too sweet, I wondered why, after all those years, Mr. Linh had got it into his head to call my brother's house and ask for my mother, then relay to me a story that had seemed well-buried. That night passed without my finding an answer. More and more, my mother's life resembled a treasure trove of questions that led to nowhere.

8 Sài Gòn

I had found that notebook in the room where my mother had lived for the two weeks before the accident, in an unexpected place: stuffed inside her pillow. I had been searching for a good hour in all the drawers and corners but with no luck. The housekeeper had cleaned and then locked the room the same day my mother died. Everybody in the house was probably inclined to give such a space a wide berth. Both my brother and the housekeeper were surprised when, the day after the funeral, I asked for the key.

I took the notebook to the desk, and eagerly turned page after disintegrating page of that relic from the faraway era of subsidies, only to find in astonishment that there wasn't a single sign to prove it once belonged to my mother. But the more I thought about it, the more I was convinced that this notebook had some special meaning. Special enough for my mother to bring it with her all the way from Hà Nội, then hide it well within the stuffing of the thick pillow, and then even sew the pillowcase shut. I picked up the notebook, turned it this way and that, and finally, between the glued sheets making up its cover, I found a photograph, black-and-white and yellowed somewhat by time. In was the photograph of a young white man, with dark hair and ever so limpid eyes. And on the back of the photo, three lines, handwritten: *Paul Polotsky, 1954, 21 avenue de Suffren, Paris*. My mother's familiar hand.

I only realized that I had moved to stand at the window, lost in thought, when I registered what was unfolding across the small yard: a couple in their birthday suits struggling and tumbling from the sofa to the floor, in a living room in semidarkness. Through the window next to theirs, a younger couple was changing positions on an immense bed, movements deft and professional. Belatedly, I recognized our neighbor and her boyfriend, and on the other bed, famous faces in the X-rated industry.

9 Paris

Thursday. The group of eight was led to a round table, a table on the second floor by the window, a window overlooking the main street, a street that at nine p.m. was immersed in a silence broken only by the occasional car, whose headlights swept the unpopulated pavement. At seven fifteen, when it was time to correct homework, someone had nonchalantly suggested, "How about a bite after this." The class came alive. They discussed a possible locus for the *bite*. One place had fresh plump waitresses but dry, thin nem. Another was generous with prawns in their salad rolls but skimpy with water in their toilet tank. In the third, the nem was fresh and plump and each roll had a good two prawns and the water in the tank was always at a generous level but the owner had an especially slap-inviting face ...

Listening to those remarks, I couldn't help but think that those who want a crash course in Vietnamese cuisine in Paris would do well to consult Vietnamese language students; while those who want to study the Vietnamese language would end up learning nothing but the map of Vietnamese cuisine in Paris.

After half an hour they managed to agree on a restaurant that ticked all their boxes. But a phone call informed them that due to a hundred clay pots being detained in Le Havre port, a state of affairs that was now in its second week, the coveted clay pot–steamed chicken was regrettably absent from the menu. Another ten minutes of discussion ensued. The final verdict was: they would still go to that restaurant, they would order this and that, but they needed another phone call to check their availability before booking. This time everything went smoothly. Only twenty minutes were left for correcting homework. But now the excitement had died down. Minds were already occupied with visions of dancing delicacies. Stomachs had begun to growl.

If French television was a formidable enemy of Vietnamese language classes, Vietnamese restaurants turned out to be even more so. My students, at any rate, had choices (out of the hundreds of Vietnamese dishes, out of the dozens of French TV channels), but I, I had none but this (shop assistant-*cum*-language teacher, a day off means a day's pay deducted, half a day off the same).

At eight thirty the whole class marched to the restaurant. The one student left out, also apparently the youngest, was Luc, whose family name was unknown either to me or to the other students. No one in fact knew anything about him, and no one seemed curious to find out. He always sat in a discreet corner; he never made small talk, or raised his hand, or joined their nights out, or tagged along on the Métro, or visited any classmate's place. Back in the beginning he had indeed tried to take part in class activities, his motivation in taking this class presumably not being language learning but having something to pass the time, almost like a little club, with a few Vietnamese phrases thrown in as a bonus. Yes, more than once he'd tried to blend in with the crowd. But he would immediately be sidelined. This is a fact obvious to anybody.

The moment he walked into class, people would smirk into their hands.

When he said he was seeking a companion for a summer trip across Vietnam, they looked away and yawned.

If he showed off a raw silk scarf he had bought for a female colleague's upcoming birthday, a snigger would be heard: Ah, is it her fiftieth? Or sixtieth?

A girl in the class got married and invited everyone but him. He somehow found out and asked to contribute to the group gift, but they refused, saying everything had already been arranged, he should just give his own present to the happy couple. He was, of course, absent at the event, where every seat was marked with a name card.

When Tết came around, he timidly ventured that if we were to have a celebration, he knew a shop that sells bánh tét cylindrical cakes and head cheese flown straight from the producer, they used Vietnam Airlines and thus ran no risk of being detained in Le Havre. He was met with indifference.

That very night, the students went out to eat together, and passed a resolution to put their collective foot down regarding *that dude Luc*, whose mere face seemed to dampen every gathering.

He seemed to catch on right away. Since that day, he took to huddling in a corner. I found it puzzling that he kept coming to the class. When the Chinese class started upstairs, he signed up immediately. At first, he seemed elated. He wore a new, confident air to the Vietnamese class, waving his Chinese textbooks around. In the ten-minute break he would work on his Chinese homework, reading it aloud, it was hard to say whether to save time or to impress others. But no one seemed to notice. Weeks passed, until he no longer did anything during the breaks but sat and bit his fingernails, his face turned to the ground. Apprehensive, I kept expecting him to either burst into tears or jump up and hit someone. But nothing ever happened. He just kept showing up week after week, right on time, and gingerly sought out the seat in a discreet corner. One day, running into me at the Métro station, the Chinese teacher remarked: "*That dude Luc* is an oddball for sure, he used to spend the ten-minute break working on his Vietnamese homework, he even read it out loud, but now he just sits and bites his fingernails in a corner." I imagined how he had also tried to take part in the activities of the Chinese class, and had been immediately sidelined. The students of that class had also passed a resolution to put their collective foot down regarding *that dude Luc*, whose mere face seemed to dampen every gathering.

The group of eight decided that each would pick a dish for them all to share, then order more if they were still hungry. In high spirits, they told the waiter to bring each of them a cup of white liquor to wet their anticipating lips. All in all, a great show of camaraderie. The waiter even gave them a complimentary dish of prawn crackers and a bowl of pickled glittering chives, then winked at me: "Hey Hanoian, have ya been over here for long?"

The students looked at one another. The most studious woman of the class groaned, Vietnamese was such an impossibly hard language, she'd studied and studied and all she could pick out from that utterance was *Hanoi*. A man of astonishingly short stature, eager to display his connoisseurship, jumped in to explain: the reason it's so hard is that the waiter has a Southern accent. Even his girlfriend, *a rooted Hanoian*, when she came to visit him in Sài Gòn, could only understand half what was said, she had to ask his interpreter to explain the other half to her. The others looked at him, approvingly. He himself looked at me, stealthily. Once, over a year ago, he came to me after class when all the others had left, asking for my help with a letter. A curt letter in an illegible scrawl and full of spelling mistakes. After much deciphering, I managed to make out that the writer was imploring him to send money home urgently so she had money to pay her rent and money for her phone bill and money to buy her scooter back from the pawnshop. He listened as I read it through, then with an embarrassed blush said that *his girl* was actually a very frugal hard worker, she had few *material* needs, without her familial obligations she surely wouldn't have needed him to provide *financial* help. I took notice of the lengths he went to avoid the word *money*, the very word that danced and capered throughout the letter. Then he took from his chest pocket an A4-size sheet of paper, folded twice, a typed reply that he had already prepared in advance and wanted me to help translate asap. When we reached the Métro station he was deep in thought, then before getting onto the train he gave me an embarrassed glance and asked me to please keep *this thing* secret for him, because he was still in the midst of divorce proceedings and his lawyer had told him not to breathe a word about it. Later, I helped him with translations a few more times, mostly from Vietnamese to French, because at the other end *his girl* had found someone who could translate his letters for her. Relieved, I wanted to ask why *his girl* didn't ask them to translate her letters before sending them to France, but I thought better of it. The letters from *his girl* were presumably his only reason for attending my Vietnamese classes.

The waiter brought the students' orders one by one, the last being coal–roast beef, a marvel to behold. To the guests' shouts of admiration, flames burst from the pan in his hand. The whole room turned to look, then someone clapped, and everyone else followed, I didn't know to what imaginary melody but was reminded of the revolutionary song *Let's fan the flame, we fight the Yanks* that was once a staple of the loudspeakers in Thành Công Ward. The waiter set the pan down in the middle of the table and looked at me, beaming proudly: "Betcha don't have this in Hà Nội!" My students glanced at one another; again, all they had caught was the word *Hanoi*.

They tried the dishes one by one and lavished praise upon them. Not one to miss a chance to display his connoisseurship, Shorty explained that when it came to Vietnamese cuisine, no place could rival Noisy-le-Grand, where the offerings were as delicious as they were cheap, the only catch being you had to go quite a tricky distance. So what if it was quite a tricky distance, said the middle-aged woman in front of him, there was a global recession going on, a dime saved is a dime earned. She finished by huffing like a rhinoceros. Dead silence all around. They hadn't forgotten the lesson last December on the theme of jobs, when a question was asked of everybody: What's your profession? Do you love your job? They all chimed in excitedly, and *that dude Luc* was even so bold as to venture a whole speech. But the middle-aged woman, visibly upset, refused to speak in Vietnamese; she launched into a diatribe in French: "What's my job? My job is lining up for unemployment benefits, that's my job. Because while you fortunate kids can go to your jobs to pleasure yourselves, my job laid me off yesterday. Hehehehe, just like that, the HR executive snatched himself a floozy from wherever and a month later he served me with a letter saying my contract was up and the company couldn't afford to renew it." At that, she burst into tears. Dead silence all around. That wasn't the first time she had tried to provoke, to set herself against the others. Just a few weeks before, during a lesson on family, she told of how her own little family consisted of *this little baby boy*, just one month old, a true bundle of cuteness. They were all startled speechless. Then someone piped up boldly: "What a keeper your husband is, looking after your son so that the missus can go practice her Vietnamese!" She burst into hysterical laughter, saying, husband and son her ass, it was this pup that she had just adopted, and then, totally deadpan, "What a bunch of gullible kids you are!" Regardless of the language in which a question was put to her, she would hurl back her reply in her mother tongue. Every time, I asked myself why she wasted her money on a language class. Singles mixers can be found in every corner of Paris. She could easily net some dozens of single men if she wanted. There were indeed a few single men in my class, but they were only interested in being netted by a Vietnamese woman. But the middle-aged woman seemed unable to grasp that fact, and after two years she was still paying to provoke the class with her sobbing tears or hysterical laughter.

I had a hunch that a confrontation was now unavoidable. The middle-aged woman was giving off that formidable battle-ready vibe of a rhinoceros suffering from aggressive depression. On this day, and I didn't know if it was deliberate or not, she was wearing a light gray dress, revealing a fleshy pair of thighs in stockings also of a light gray color, and her hair was gathered into a mini horn on her forehead. It's said that nothing can stand the rhino's mighty wrath, and that the single-horned type is the most fearsome of them all.

Shorty again resumed his travelogue of Vietnam, a pretense to talk about *his girl,* whom he asserted to be *a rooted Hanoian.* The others showed no interest in that claim. *Rooted Hanoian* or *transplanted Hanoian,* it was less important than bánh bột lọc tapioca dumplings with prawns or bánh cuốn rice sheets with ground pork. The eight dishes were swiftly wiped clean. On to another discussion, to decide on a few more dishes to eat with anything-goes fried rice to give the night a satisfying end. Braised pork? Braised fish? Stir-fried greens? Don't forget to ask for another bowl of lime chili fish sauce. The show of camaraderie was still going strong. But the middle-aged woman seemed to have had enough. Looking at no one in particular, she tossed out this verdict: "Should have ordered the twelve euro set and been done with it, three dishes guarantee a full belly until tomorrow, and a complimentary iced coffee on top of that!" Dead silence all around. Since the day she'd told the class about her puppy, her words never failed to be met with dead silence.

Tonight's silence was also tinged with a certain anxiety: the students shared my apprehension that Rhino was looking for someone to unleash the full might of her wrath. Only innocent Shorty was oblivious, talking and laughing away. With his mouth open wide, and wearing a jade green suit glimmering with golden threads, which looked expensive but also the wrong size, he bore a striking resemblance to a bullfrog. He waved the middle-aged woman's verdict away and told them just to eat according to their need and pay according to their ability, he would take care of the rest. Everybody rejoiced, the middle-aged woman shook her single horn, and Shorty proceeded with his Vietnam travelogue. From then on he monopolized the conversation. He seemed willing to pay for the right to talk about *his girl*. He needed to confide in someone about *this thing*. This Vietnamese language class was the only place he could do so without much potential harm. At his place, at his friends' places, at his workplace, at every public place, he must keep his lips zipped, because his lawyer had told him not to breathe a word about *this thing*. I sat right next to him, so I got a numbing earful of his plan to retire and build a new life with Ms. *Dinh Nguyen Thi*. I made a few vain attempts at imagining Mr. Shorty and Ms. Dinh hand in hand, walking to a tai chi group by Hoàn Kiếm Lake, but my stubborn brain kept picturing a green bullfrog a meter and a half tall, and the youngest daughter of my brother's housekeeper, a girl with chemically straightened hair in a modernized áo dài, the way she'd looked in that photograph the housekeeper had thrust into my hand the day I was to come back to France, insisting that "if you know some Westerner in need of company, please send him to my little Dinh in Hải Dương."

Shorty's story should have come to a safe denouement, but he ended with a sensational revelation:

"But my girl and I have never done the business!"

The chopsticks stopped rattling. The middle-aged woman leaped out of her seat:

"So what the heck did you do? Sniff each other's armpits? Did you skimp on your Viagra?"

Now the confrontation began in earnest. They were facing each other; she, big-bodied, was standing, and he, short in stature, was sitting; a remarkable picture of a rhino about to grab at a bullfrog. Yet Shorty didn't seem to be angry. He swallowed a gulp of water, then announced gallantly, as if he wanted everybody to hear:

"We decided that, during our engagement, we wouldn't do the business!"

The middle-aged woman was now positively panting, her mini-horn wiggling:

"Away with those lame excuses. Just admit that you *can't* do it!"

Shorty swallowed another gulp of water, and then declared, with all the pride he could muster:

"She's still a virgin!"

"Listen to this madman!"

The middle-aged woman guffawed, and some others seemed to laugh with her. Shorty just sat there, crimson-faced and silent. After a while, perhaps offended that none among those present had spoken a word in his defense, he looked from face to face and suddenly hurled out:

"I'll tell you the truth, I'm so done with that stupid rule of yours, that once a man and a woman get together they have to go at it like rabbits."

No one reacted, except to look down and resume clicking their chopsticks. The declaration should have touched a few romantic souls, if only Shorty had been a slightly more robust man. He got to his feet, picked up his briefcase, and left without a word. Below the jade green suit pants, the matching shoes looked shiny and fancy, but also the wrong size.

The hilarity died down instantly. The seven faces looked at one another in awkward dismay. The seven sets of despair began to rise from the thought of that bill, which must have bloomed sevenfold since Shorty declared that they *pay according to their ability,* after which another twenty dishes had graced the table, dishes with dubious belly-filling capacity but all such marvels to behold that the waiter was always greeted with hearty applause.

Not until the most studious woman cleared her throat and asked the waiter for the bill, and also for a calculator to facilitate their going dutch, did the whole class learn that Shorty had already put it all on his credit card. The seven mouths stretched into gaping smiles. On the way to the Métro station, someone asked:

"What does that fella do to be rolling in such *dough*?"

Someone else answered:

"Sales executive, he wields make-or-break power in his company!"

The middle-aged woman, triumphantly:

"Told you so, all executives are infatuated with a floozy!"

Dead silence all around until we parted ways.

After switching lines, I somehow ended up sitting behind two of my students, who were still ardently discussing Shorty's line of work. The first, wearing a stung look, insisted that the whole story needed further verification, because that bullfrog could work for a million years and never get to the executive level, the speaker knew this because he had books to back him up, or rather this one book that he had just finished, a very smart book, *How the Chinese Tell Your Fortune from Your Face,* which maintains that a short stature is fortune's worst enemy.

The other shook his head, you should see an executive meeting at his company, a squad of squatting bullfrogs, and every single one a big shot.

The first, at a loss for any counterargument, bitterly accepted the truth that this bullfroggy big shot was the only one in the class with enough *dough* to fund several trips a year to Vietnam.

Not noticing his companion's tone, the second continued with his joke:

"When they arrive in Vietnam, all bullfrogs turn into rhinos."

Still sounding stung, the first exclaimed:

"But what the heck does he need to go to Vietnam for if not to do the business?"

The second was lost in contemplation for a while, and then echoed with much indignation:

"True, what the heck do you need to go to Vietnam for if not to do the business??"

And then both got up and left the train, leaving me alone to consider that in all likelihood, Shorty had finalized his divorce that morning, hence he let his tongue run loose about *his girl* and inviting the whole class out to celebrate. If it hadn't been for the confrontation with the middle-aged woman then who knows, maybe he would have gone on to invite them to his wedding in Vietnam—they could pay according to their ability, he would cover the rest of the ticket fees. Perhaps that very afternoon, he had stood in the middle of the courthouse (in that jade green suit two sizes too large), looked from face to face in the jury, then suddenly hurled out: "I'll tell you the truth, I'm so done with that rule of yours, that once a man and a woman get married, they have to spend a lifetime together!" His lawyer would have been stunned. His wife also would have been stunned, before turning on the tap of her tears (she, too, was in a light gray dress, revealing a fleshy pair of thighs, her hair gathered into a mini-horn on her forehead). The audience would have been sympathetic. Even a rhino has the right to suffer. When the court session was over, the wife took her lawyer aside and asked:

"The old dog takes several trips a year to Vietnam, what do you think he's doing there?"

"What the heck is there to do in Vietnam if not the business?" the lawyer snapped.

"But he's impotent!" the wife insisted.

"There's such a thing as Viagra," the lawyer smirked.

Again the tap turned on.

When I got home that evening, the clock already read eleven. Mike had been picked up from kindergarten by my neighbor and was now sleeping on the sofa, his hands balled into fists, the TV beside him blaring an episode of CSI, Not Suitable for Children Under Twelve.

10 Paris

On my twentieth birthday, I decided to ask my mother about my biological father. My reasoning was thus: a person should know who begot them. My mother was totally taken by surprise, because the topic had never come up before. She refused to engage, saying all that was in the past, there was no point bringing it up now. But I persisted. I promised, whatever the truth, it wouldn't drive a wedge between us. And I waxed philosophical about how at the age of twenty I was now mature enough to face the truth, and at any rate I didn't believe any paternal bond could exist between those who had never spent a single day together. Finally, my mother gave in. But all she could tell me was the name of the man who was supposed to be my birth father. "Paul Polotsky."

Bill paused. I was startled. Coincidences were, it turned out, not that hard to come by. When the telephone rang yesterday, I'd had to listen to the silence at the other end for quite a while. Assuming it was a wrong number, I was about to hang up when a man's voice said he wanted to see me, not for a space in the Vietnamese language class, but to discuss someone named Paul Polotsky. I woke up startled a few times in the night, nagged by the sense that I shouldn't have accepted so readily, that I should've at least asked how he'd got wind about the link between me and Polotsky, a link I was confident that Polotsky himself didn't know.

The only thing I knew about the caller was a naked first name: Bill. Bill as in President Clinton. An all-American name in my book.

On the Métro, the thought crossed my mind that Bill would change his mind and call off the meeting he himself suggested. Or alternatively, that he would show up on time and right off the bat demand that I cease following Polotsky, otherwise the old man would sue me or perhaps set some thugs on me. I shivered a little. Finally, to quiet those misgivings, I told myself that there was only one way this Bill could've discovered that I'd been stalking Polotsky: if he and I were following the same target.

The café had emptied a little now. The patrons were here mostly for lunch. The tables strewn with dirty plates and empty bottles. Exhausted waiters, after running like whirlwinds for the better part of an hour, collected cutlery while yawning and wiping their sweat with their shirt sleeves.

Bill came straight over to where I was sitting but didn't greet me or offer his hand. After standing there for a few seconds, he automatically sat down on the other chair and stared at me. But I was neither surprised nor annoyed. This uncivil coldness was familiar to me from Mr. Linh. If my mother's old acquaintance had been a black bronze statue, I was now faced with a plaster one (he was an all-white apparition, white clothes and white scarf and white-blond hair). His stare was no different from Mr. Linh's a few months ago. A few months ago, in the small living room off that small alley in a corner of Sài Gòn, I'd looked in vain at the wall on which there was neither a picture, nor a frame, nor even a stain to distract me from that stare. Now I just sighed and looked out onto the street. A street bathed in gold. A great thunderstorm had passed over Paris in the early morning, sweeping it clean of all the heat that had accumulated since the beginning of summer. I hadn't been to this café since time beyond memory. Last night, when Bill asked me where we could meet, I said the name of the first place that popped into my mind. I regretted it as soon as it was out of my mouth, but Bill had already agreed and hung up.

Since time beyond memory I hadn't been here, hadn't sat by this window from which I could look down at the street or up at the rolling roofs. The last time I'd been here, I discovered a bird cage on a plane tree, close to the lowest roof. The last time I'd been here, I said nothing to Kai. For a while before we parted ways, Kai was always angry, for reasons I could not fathom. One midsummer's day, he texted me from his family's vacation home: "I don't want to pursue this relationship anymore." Another week went by, and I wanted to text back: "Will you please be quiet, please?" But I was the one who kept quiet.

The street was bathed in brilliant gold. In that golden sheen, unmistakably June-esque, I heard Bill's monotonous voice recounting how on his twentieth birthday he'd decided to ask his mother about his biological father, but all that she could tell him was the name Paul Polotsky. It had been a quick and spontaneous liaison, they didn't know anything about each other and had no intention of intertwining their lives. And condoms and contraceptives hadn't been as ubiquitous back then. Bill found the name immediately in the Paris phone book, the only Paul Polotsky in all the phone books of France. He had a hunch that this was his father. He dialed the number. The phone rang three times; a voice answered. A man's voice, which sent chills down his spine. Bill composed himself and explained that he was looking for a man of this name, and if it was the right man, could they please talk. The voice on the other end hesitated but agreed. With all the courage he could muster, Bill uttered the words he had practiced a million times in his mind: "I don't suppose you know about me, Pa, but I'm your son."

Dead silence on the other end. Bill continued, "I won't cause you any trouble. I just want to know that you exist. Today is my twentieth birthday." He waited in silence. After a few moments the other end spoke, expressing happiness to hear that Bill had turned twenty, surprise at the discovery of a son so grown up, and explaining that he'd had no contact with the girl after their brief encounter. Bill said that he didn't blame his father, that no one was at fault, that he was perfectly happy living with his single mom because she was the most wonderful mom in the world... and so on and so forth, his words pouring out in a torrent. As if he had been mute for years. He remembered saying, "Maybe it's what Mom wanted, Pa." He had prepared himself for this, but uttering that "Pa" for the first time in his life stirred up tremendous emotions in him. Finally, he told the man that he had some errand in Paris in the next few days, his first time visiting the capital, so if it wasn't too much trouble could they please meet, maybe at some café, just for half an hour or so. "I won't cause you any trouble. I just want to know that you exist," he said again. The man concurred, and gave him the address of a café that was said to be peaceful.

For the next few nights Bill dreamed of Paul Polotsky, and though he didn't know what the old man looked like, he had a vision of a man small in stature, with dark hair, an air of timidity and dreaminess, and the fabled *Russian soul.*

He dreamed that the old man took him to a small village, a *Quiet Flows the Don* affair, where the villagers threw them a welcome feast and gave him his first ever taste of pork bun and kvass, and he danced with a charming young woman who was the spitting image of Aksinia. He was still giddy upon waking up. At that moment, "Paul Polotsky" seemed the most beautiful name in the world. He lamented that he couldn't claim that Russian cognomen, and wondered why his mother had given her only son such an all-American first name. He even tried to frankenstein up a name, which left him frustrated: Bill Polotsky simply sounded too off-putting.

On the much-anticipated day, he boarded a plane to Paris, then took the Métro to the café, an hour early. He was indeed agitated; the errand he had talked about was just an excuse for this rendezvous. He sat down at the most discreet table in the least crowded corner, chin in hand and eyes on the door, hoping to catch a glimpse of Polotsky the moment the old man walked in. Bill had in his pocket a full pack of tissues, knowing that their very first greetings would reduce him to blubbering. He knew he was breaking his promise to his mother. But the paternal bond was undeniably sacred.

Half an hour passed. Then another half an hour. Two hours past the agreed-upon time, Polotsky was still nowhere to be seen. The café was indeed peaceful, since Bill arrived there had been only a few other patrons, three men already with company, another drunk as a skunk, and finally a youth constantly sucking on his cigarette.

"My patience had run out, I got out my phone and dialed his number, but I was in for a nasty shock: the phone operator's voice saying this number was no longer in use. I tried again, again the operator's voice. After the third try, I was forced to accept the truth."

For the whole duration of Bill's story, I felt like I was listening to a foreign language tape. But then I told myself it was precisely this monotonous, sleep-inducing voice that prevented his interlocutor from shedding tears for him. The thought crossed my mind that perhaps last night Bill had locked himself in his room, telling and retelling this story a dozen times, at first sobbing and sniveling as he spoke, then sneering and swearing, and then finally reaching a stone-faced fluency. He had stared at me for so long without a word before beginning, presumably to rehearse it in his head a few more times. And the result was incredible: he managed to tell his own story as if it was someone else's. Even the few words exchanged on the phone last night must've been well rehearsed, spoken in the same monotonous, detached tone that knocked me so off-balance I automatically agreed to meet him, automatically gave him the name of this café that somehow popped into my mind.

In a contest for cold fish, I thought, Bill and Mr. Linh would share the first prize. Mr. Linh wanted to convince me that the *fatal obsession* that my mother had aroused in him years ago had long vanished, and Bill wanted to impress on me that the same had happened to the *tremendous emotions* that Polotsky had once agitated in his chest. But it also struck me that Bill had inadvertently added more difficulty to my own quest for Polotsky: after being called out of the blue by a stranger claiming to be his son, Polotsky, now presumably with a family of his own, had attempted to avoid trouble by hiding his home number. For the last twenty years, he had been paying an annual fee to France Télécom to have his details withdrawn from the phone books.

Back in Paris, ten days after my mother's funeral, I'd consulted the phone books and searched high and low, first in Paris proper and the banlieues, then throughout the twenty-four regions of France, but no Paul Polotsky could be found. Back then he had not yet started teaching at the Department of Eastern European Studies. Putting his name into search engines only yielded a few vague bits of news, a few institutes where he had once been a visiting lecturer, years ago, for a laughably short term, and on an outdated topic, such that no one I called had even bothered to look in their records. One secretary told me flatly that in that era before the digital revolution, it wasn't as though people could store *any old nonsense* in the virtual warehouses that they did today. I spent the next few weeks traipsing between countless hotels and post offices to ask for their old phone books. A journey through Paris and the twenty-four regions of France by way of two hundred phone books, and there was still no trace of my quarry. I spent the next few weeks listing, as a very last resort, every single Polotsky from those two hundred phone books, hoping against the odds that one would be related to mine.

* *

When you're an immigrant you learn not to give up too soon. After exhausting the phone books, I had determined that in the whole of France in the last ten years there were but nine Mr. Polotskys listed, but all changed their addresses and numbers every two or three years, apart from a certain Anatole who had stayed put for the last five. Some appeared out of the blue, perhaps a tender-aged person moving out of their parents' home, or a middle-aged person newly divorced, or a whatever-aged person fresh off the Russian boat. Some vanished into thin air, which perhaps meant six feet under, or into a nursing home, or back to their long-separated homeland, or into the home of a new spouse, or simply that they had ditched the landline to wholly embrace the mobile world, as single French folks were increasingly doing. I had no recourse left but to call them up one by one, moving down the list alphabetically. Even the most seasoned private eye, I reasoned, must resort to such low-tech methods.

In the end, these nine gentlemen cost me several dozen phone calls, all beginning with the same question: *Please can you tell me if this is Mr. Paul Polotsky's residence?* roughly half concluding with the person on the other end hanging up without even a response, after which I would wait a few days before calling again, and a few days more if the second call went the same way of the first. Three strikes and I'm out, I promised myself. Some calls only lasted half a minute, just enough time for my opening question to be met with a succinct *Sorry, wrong number*. Some lasted a good hour, which I spent in apprehension of my next phone bill, but the elderly man on the other end, deathly bored, was in need of someone to pour his heart out to, he might not be Paul Polotsky but he was also a Russian émigré, constantly tormented by nostalgia for his country and a lifetime of memories. One call made me laugh, when a woman squawked: "Paul, you good-for-nothing, it's another chick asking you to the dance hall." Another threatened to make me cry, when a girl sobbed: "Who are you? Don't you know Paul passed away last year, the day before his thirtieth birthday?" But the strangest call went like this:

"Please can you tell me if this is Mr. Paul Polotsky's residence?"

"An American already called to ask for a Paul Polotsky this morning. What do you want?"

"I just want to know if Mr. Paul Polotsky lives there."

"Be honest with me: the Chinese immigrant mafia are after those deeds, yes?"

"What deeds?"

"The title deeds that your Qing lords drew up with our Tsar."

"I don't know what you're talking about."

"Cut the crap. You lost those deeds in your war with the Japs and now you're so desperate to find them again, you've even asked the CIA for help."

"What deeds are you talking about?"

"You played a trick on our Tsar and picked up our four islands to the east of the Amur for a song."

"The Amur in remote Siberia?"

"What other Amur is there?"

"This is the first time I'm hearing about these deeds."

"Cut the crap. You have been scheming for the whole last century."

"And what does the 13th arrondissement mafia have to do with it?"

"You have just announced a hundred-million-buck reward to anyone who finds the deeds."

"And what does Paul Polotsky have to do with it?"

I still don't know why the person on the other end chose this point to hang up. After that the line went busy, and the following day the number went dead. I'd tried a few days before and was still met with the operator's voice. Now, face to face with Bill, it suddenly occurred to me that he was likely the one who had called that morning: after twenty years tormented by questions, he must have reignited his search for his birth father. The first thing he did was to ransack the phone books of Paris and the twenty-four regions of France to make a list of every single Polotsky there was, hoping against the odds that one would be related to his (and by extension to Bill himself). After arriving at the names of those nine gentlemen, Bill had dialed their numbers one by one, moving systematically down the list. His reasoning was along the same lines as mine: even the most seasoned private eye has to resort to such low-tech methods. In short, he and I had inadvertently made the same calculations and engaged in the same basic search operations. Then one day both of us arrived at the same number, asked the same question about Paul Polotsky, and roused the same suspicion on the other end, that we were after the title deeds of those four islands on the Amur, with him an agent of the CIA (judging by his all-American name) and me of the Chinese mafia (judging by my decidedly Asian accent).

Leaving Bill at the café, I went to Mike's kindergarten. The boy turned five and a half today. Five years and six months ago, at this very hour, I was rolled out of the operating room to go and lie in the post-op, drifting in and out of dreams, with a painful void in my belly. I had only had a few minutes to clasp that bloody, wrinkly creature to my breast, while thinking up a name to tell those who were registering it and writing it down on his wristband. I had no immediate answer. After a few moments I breathed, "Mai." "Mike?" they repeated. Astonished, I nodded. "Mike." Mike, I was already beginning to love that name. That whole night, I lay hugging Mike in the gloomy darkness of that hospital, where from time to time a startled newborn cried sharply before total silence reigned once more.

At Tân Sơn Nhất airport, I had wanted to tell my brother Mai the origin of my son Mike's name, but I quickly realized that it was not the place to tell such things, and that I wouldn't have known how to even if it was. My brother quickly began calling my son Michael. All his men called him Michael Jackson. Perhaps nobody knew, and it was the first time I myself noticed, that the boy shares not only his family name, but even his first name with my brother. My brother who lived with me under a roof for ten years, the very first ten years of my life.

11 Hà Nội

It is a truth universally acknowledged, that your local police in Vietnam have better and more detailed knowledge about your life than you do yourself.

If not for them I would never have learned, that day so long ago, that my eldest uncle had come to Hà Nội with his family so that my grandparents could meet them for the first time.

I got home from school just in time to see the local policeman pick up his briefcase and move to the door. On the table, the tea had grown cold in two cups, untouched. My mother seemed cheerful. Hovering on the threshold as she saw the policeman out, she was still telling anecdotes.

She told of her party committee's meeting, and of shouting slogans cheering on our counteroffensive at the Cambodian border.

She told of her local civil unit meeting, and of criticizing the bad elements who engaged in individualistic private business.

She told of her department's model workers' meeting, and of advocating for the Good People Doing Good Deeds movement.

For those few minutes, she played three successive roles: Mrs. Deputy Secretary of the Party Committee, Mrs. Vice Head of the Local Civil Unit, Mrs. Head of the University Subdepartment. Three roles equally inflamed with revolutionary, optimistic passion. But I knew it was only an act. The moment her chief audience (the local policeman) was gone, her face sunk, and she sat back on her chair as still as a statue.

After a while, my father walked in. The tension was palpable.

My mother, raising her voice: "Sit down. We need to talk."

My father sat down on the chair opposite hers.

My mother, indicating the tea already cold in the two cups, untouched: "It's about your family."

My father said nothing.

On our block, my parents were often cited as the exemplary couple living in harmony, the reason being one would always keep silent when the other raised their voice. I thought it was as good a reason as any, though the voice raiser was more often than not my mother, and the silent one, my father. Mrs. Socialist New Wife, performed for twenty years opposite my father, was perhaps my mother's most iconic role.

My mother: "Your eldest brother worked for the impostor government."

My father said nothing.

My mother: "Your eldest brother had to go to reeducation."

My father said nothing.

My mother: "Your eldest brother's daughter has been arrested many times for attempting to cross the border."

My father said nothing.

My mother: "The local police were here."

My father was startled. His face sunk.

That night, my brother and I had dinner on our own. Rice bulked out with noodles, boiled morning glory, pan-roasted peanuts. My parents had taken their bicycles and left, each going their own way.

Later, I would come to learn that at that time, my mother had recently applied for a fellowship in France. The entire Ministry of Education was allotted only three fellowships, for which there were ninety applicants, all French-teaching cadres from the three regions of the country. This one-to-thirty ratio was cause for consternation. My mother lost points on professional competence but gained some when it came to her personal history. Those were the days when personal history still trumped competence. In the Ministry's reasoning, the imperialistic US was still public enemy number one of the Vietnamese people, and France was a US ally, so one would have to have a rock-solid personal history in order not to be swayed by the ally of the enemy. After multiple rounds of vetting, my mother's application had finally dropped on the desk of the head of the Bureau of Training and International Cooperation. The final test was to be the judgement of her local police. If all went well, my mother would be among the first academics from the Socialist Republic of Vietnam on fellowships in France. But the arrival of my eldest uncle's family had thrown it all into jeopardy.

Later, I would also come to learn that before Liberation Day, my eldest uncle had been an accountant in a small Sài Gòn bank. His salary was no better than that of a civil servant. The family's main source of income was his wife's little sewing shop in Đa Kao Ward. They had a big family, but all the children were given a good education. The elder ones went on to study overseas. The three youngest stayed home with my uncle and aunt. A run-of-the-mill middle-class family in the city. April 1975 came, the bank closed down, and my uncle found himself cooling his heels at home. After a month, the new government sent him for two weeks of reeducation. Next came more heel cooling. Naturally, the new government's banks had no need for former employees with his kind of personal history. So the whole family lived on what the little sewing shop could bring in. But their biggest concern was their fourth daughter, Đức. Ever since Liberation Day, my cousin Đức had harbored just one desire: to get out. Ten times she tried to cross the border, and ten times she failed: each time, the boat would be discovered by the border guards before it could even depart, and each time would cost her three taels of gold and three months in prison. After those ten times, Đức had become familiar with most prisons from South to North. After those ten times, my uncle and aunt came close to selling their house to settle the debts she'd incurred. After those ten times, for a long time, Đức acted the vexed hermit. She cooled her heels at home, reading martial arts novels alongside my uncle. The two of them on two cots, and between them, a pile of Jin Yong books and another pile of takeout rice meals, half-eaten. She had encountered Jin Yong in Chí Hòa prison, in the form of a handwritten copy made by a fellow inmate who had committed the whole volumes-long story to memory. At first, she read to while away the time, but soon she was hooked. Immediately after being released, she combed all the lice from her hair, got a proper wash, and then went to a bookstore to rent a pile of Jin Yong novels. She got my uncle hooked on them too. She didn't go out to see anyone. She wasn't pretty, was tough as a man, and her marital future seemed doomed. My aunt could only sigh and wring her hands.

But Đức was as bright as she was tough. When Đổi Mới was launched toward the end of the eighties she burnt all her martial arts novels, put away her cot, and hatched a veritable rags-to-riches scheme. Her elder brothers sent home capitalist money. She imported foreign goods and sold them for twice the price. Half of all the American grapes, La Vache Qui Rit cheese, and Italian wine sold in Bến Thành market originated from her. She built hotels to rent out to foreign tourists. She set up companies to service those who wanted to go overseas for work or study. She partnered with eastern European Việt kiều to start a textile factory in Bình Chánh. She represented western European Việt kiều in opening a leather shoe factory in Đồng Nai. She bought and sold real estate. She owned an array of villas. But for all of that, she was still single. Some men approached her. Her parents urged her to pick one. But she turned them all down. The rumor was that she kept young lovers. College kids who needed money for their studies. Good-looking, honest-seeming boys from poor families. She was generous. Her cousins who sought a new life in

Sài Gòn all received support from her. My brother Mai, testing the waters of the business world after throwing away the math and physics contract with Cần Thơ University, also ran to her for help.

Recently, after my mother arrived in Sài Gòn, Đức bought her a three-day trip to Bangkok, flying business class and staying in a five-star hotel. She said she'd got it half-price so it cost even less than a domestic holiday in Vietnam. My mother cheerfully went on the trip. Not present to witness their conversations, I wondered if, in front of Đức, my mother had played the part of the kind, all-forgiving cadre from the North.

But all that happened years later. Back in 1977, my cousin Đức was still my parents' most hated enemy. The visit from the local policeman threw my parents off balance for months. At dinner, my brother and I would look at one another in silence. He went grocery shopping and cooked. I washed the dishes and swept the house. On the table, evening after evening: rice bulked out with noodles, boiled morning glory, pan-roasted peanuts.

My mother took her bicycle and went her own way.

My father took his bicycle and went his own way.

My mother visited her connections and asked them to put in a word for her.

My father visited his connections and asked them to put in a word for him.

My mother's and father's connections took their bicycles and went their own ways, visiting their own connections and asking them to put in a word.

The local police remained oh so distant.

We waved goodbye to our valuable possessions one by one. The black-and-white Sony TV set went first, then the Hitachi refrigerator, both secondhand from Sài Gòn flea market that had traveled on the Thống Nhất, cradled in my father's lap after two conferences of educators from the Southern provinces. That was the beauty of the train of unification: the Southerners got their long-lost brotherhood, and the Northerners, their long-sought brothers' goods.

Silver strands began to pepper my father's hair. Wrinkles furrowed my mother's face. They stopped sleeping together. My mother still slept on their bed, but my father now slept on a sedge mat on the floor. Winter began to give way to summer, and in that interim season of oppressive humidity, water ran in streams across the floor, but my parents remained steadfastly separated. Anxiety could kill any inkling of desire. But my parents' solidarity could survive any degree of separation. They played the part of good comrades. Many nights I woke up wondering where and when they found a moment to discuss their anxieties, their connections. The anxieties of that time were very different from those of today. And the connections of that time were also different from those of today. The connections of that time accepted the meters of cloth or cans of powdered milk that we had to offer. Those of today will only take dollar bills.

The day my mother got her approval from the Ministry, my parents didn't dare tell anyone. The day she departed for France, the whole block was still in the dark, and my brother and I were none the wiser. Day after day my brother went grocery shopping and cooked, I swept the house and washed the dishes, and my father walked around the house like a zombie. Three creatures keeping to their own corners. How I wished the black-and-white Sony had still been there for us to gather around, even if only for a couple of hours before sleep. How I wished the Hitachi fridge had remained in the now deserted corner, so that I could come home from school and suck on some ice while dreaming of ice cream.

After a week, the transnational train arrived in Moskva with my mother on it. Only when she sent a telegraph home, a plane ticket to France already in her pocket, did my father inform her parents. As for his own parents, neither my father or my mother had seen them since my eldest uncle's family arrived in Hà Nội. As for my father's other siblings, he hadn't seen them since then either. And the rest of the relatives and acquaintances, who lived far away, never learned my mother had been away until she was already on the way home.

The day she came home, my father went to Hàng Cỏ station to pick her up. He brought her home on his bicycle, the two of them playing the role a couple reunited after three months apart. A cyclo traveled beside them. On it were a bicycle and a scooter, still in their original packaging, the Peugeot labels loud and proud. These two representatives from France were then displayed in pomp and splendor in the middle of our living room, with the outer packaging removed but the styrofoam still intact around frames and wheels. My mother brought gifts of chocolates, raisins, face towels, and handkerchiefs for the connections who'd put in a word for her. Only the chocolates were products of France; the raisins had been bought in the USSR, and the handkerchiefs in China. The connections of that time hadn't yet learned to be too fastidious about capitalist vs. socialist wares.

Another month went by, and my parents called in a dealer to sell the scooter. Yet another month went by, and they purchased another TV set and refrigerator, new and shiny but made in the GDR. They put what was left in a savings account. Yet another few months went by, the first national currency revaluation came down catastrophically upon us, my parents managed to hoard a few dozen kilos of rice purchased at black market prices but I don't know if they were left with much, enough to afford Tết offerings to all those connections who'd put in a word for her, or a few kilos of meat and a dozen kilos of rice for each month after that. When the dust had settled, all that was left to show for my mother's fellowship in France was the Peugeot bicycle.

My parents divorced two years after that. As a ten-year-old, I wasn't allowed to be present in court. So I sat in my classroom and imagined my mother playing the role of Mrs. Socialist New Woman in front of the jury of the people. She put on such an excellent act, the jury of the people were so moved that they didn't see fit to raise any further questions. When the proceedings were over, my parents shook hands the way good comrades do. And the audience, both up above and down below, clapped up a storm.

Home from school that noon, during the last meal I would have with my brother for a while, how I wished there had been another trip overseas, either a capitalist or a socialist country would do, to cement the solidarity between father comrade and mother comrade.

12 Sài Gòn

Sitting opposite my brother Mai were two elderly guests, a man and a woman, *colleagues* of my mother, as the housekeeper had informed me when she opened the gates. The conversation must have been tedious. When I walked in, my brother was yawning, and the staring guests had found nothing better to do than rubbing and stroking their teacups.

Beyond the floor-to-ceiling windows of the living room, that corner of the city was on full display. In the background was Sài Gòn Port, quicksilver lights dancing on the water. To the right you could see the Notre Dame, its twin bell towers two dark horns in the night. There was heavy traffic on Lê Lợi Street. I wondered which of the streets down there was Huyền Trân Công Chúa, named after a princess and known for shop after shop of exercise wear; which was Cách Mạng Tháng Tám, the August Revolution Street several times longer than Phố Huế, the longest in Hà Nội; or Công Xã Paris, the Paris Commune Street even shorter than the tiny Tạm Thương Alley; and which was Tự Do—its name, meaning Liberty, promptly changed upon unification into General Uprising—Đồng Khởi.

Suddenly breaking the silence, my brother told me that the female guest was Mrs. Huệ, who'd been in my mother's fellowship cohort in Paris, and the man was Mr. Đỗ, her husband. Then he yawned again. I took a good long look at Mrs. Huệ, but there was no resemblance to the woman who appeared beside my mother throughout the album of photos from her time in France, which was usually hidden away in her private drawer. The photos had become ingrained in my memory as they were the first color photographs I'd ever seen, long before they became commonplace in Vietnam. It was a small album, only twenty nine-by-twelve-centimeter photographs, and in each photograph my mother was posing with a woman who she told everyone was her *colleague* from the Paris fellowship. That was over twenty years ago, and the woman's name had faded from my mind, but it could hardly be Mrs. Huệ, who was as short as the woman in the photos was tall, a height that at that time must have aroused envy in most Vietnamese men.

My brother yawned a few more times. He probably would have fallen asleep right there on the sofa if his phone hadn't suddenly roared into life. At the first ring, he seemed to jolt awake. He stood up, shook hands with his guests, invited them to stay for a *simple meal with the family,* and went out with his phone. The door snapped shut as if locking the three of us inside.

"There was another woman on the fellowship, right?" I asked, holding my breath.

"Madame Hòa, the most imposing: the tallest, holding the highest post, and with thirty-two years of Party membership behind her," Mrs. Huệ said.

Oh yes, Madame Hòa. Now I recalled that my mother had often added that her "colleague" was a university vice department head.

"Madame Hòa was an evil woman," Mr. Đỗ added.

He continued hurriedly, not waiting to see how we reacted to his statement:

"I was not a fellow. I was a Việt kiều; I've been a Việt kiều my whole life; in Laos I was a Laotian Việt kiều, and in France a French one. My Lao is good and my Vietnamese is good, but my French consists solely of bonjour and merci, so I hired myself out to an auto repair shop in a southeastern banlieue, near the Chinese quarter, where the clients were mostly Asian immigrants."

Seeing my blank look of incomprehension, Mr. Đỗ hastily explained:

"Half a year after we arrived in France, my first wife left me and our three kids. They were still young, so I began to look for someone else. But Vietnamese-French women disliked me for coming from Laos. Laotian-French women dismissed me for being Vietnamese. Khmer-French women wanted nothing to do with a Laotian-Vietnamese. I didn't dare go near Chinese-French women again. My ex-wife is only one eighth Chinese, yet she dumped me right after getting her residence card. Then, by chance, I met Huệ at the Vietnamese embassy. She'd only been in France for a week, to the day. I thought fortune had finally smiled upon me."

I was still confused when Mrs. Huệ continued:

"We are the same age. At forty-two, when we met, Đỗ was already married with kids, while I was still single and alone. After high school, I followed my brother to the front to fight the Americans, spending most of my youth in the Mekong Delta, U Minh Forest, near the Cambodian border. At thirty, after a bout of malaria, I was sent to the North to get an education. No exam was required for me to get a place in the university. No good degree needed to get a job in the faculty. No application submitted to get an apartment in the university's blocks. No interview with the Municipal Department head to get the special food ration. Cadres transferred from the South were given preferential treatment. But the government had no way to treat my chronic husbandlessness. They told me that you get used to being alone. But the longer I was alone, the more scared I got. The end of the year was always the worst. In the Hanoian chill I could pile blankets onto myself and still feel the cold. And the Northern men never had eyes for Southern girls, so I didn't spend anything on fancy clothes but more and more on blankets. Then I was picked to go to France for the fellowship, and there, by chance, I met Đỗ. He'd only been divorced for six months, to the day. I thought fortune had finally smiled upon me."

Mrs. Huệ paused, and Mr. Đỗ continued:

"I thought Huệ was the one the moment I laid eyes on her. I didn't need beauty, or youth; what I needed was a wife who would never leave me. I believe that she, too, thought I was the one the moment she laid eyes on me. She didn't need elegance, or riches; what she needed was a husband to replace all those blankets. It was so simple, what happened next between us. But Madame Hòa turned it into something complex. She'd been voted head of the three women fellows even before they departed for France. Once in Paris, she demanded the three of them live in the same room. Anywhere Huệ went, anything she did, the whole Embassy would know about it the next day. And the Embassy knew that I already had three children, and that my wife had left me but not divorced me, so technically I was still a married man. In an internal meeting of the fellows, Madame Hòa stood tall and pointed at Huệ's face as she enunciated her accusations: debauchery and liaison with a Việt kiều. What kind of Party member are you, Madame Hòa said, fresh off the boat in Paris and letting yourself be bought off by a depraved capitalist? Madame Hòa ordered Huệ to compose three accounts of self-criticism: one for the Embassy, one for the Ministry of Education and Higher Studies back home, and one for the Party committee of the university that employed her. In each account, a pledge to cease her relationship with me, under penalty of being sent home on the next flight available."

Mr. Đỗ shook his head and picked up his cup, but the tea had yet to wet his lips when Mrs. Huệ resumed:

"After that, wherever I went, Madame Hòa would be there with me. I would leave a supermarket after buying some sanitary pads, and Madame Hòa would be waiting at the door, and she would ask, pointing at my bag, were you buying presents for that Đỗ and his kids again. I would nurse a toothache for a week before finally changing trains three times to get to the dentist, and in the waiting room Madame Hòa would materialize to jerk her chin at me and ask, what are you seeing a gynecologist for. I lived in Paris for three months and not once did I see the inside of a cinema; all that I saw of the Louvre was from a passing bus, and only knew the National Library from photographs, because Madame Hòa condemned them all as capitalist culture imbecile romance. Đỗ was banned from the embassy. A week before our fellowship came to an end, I went to the university library to return my textbooks. Madame Hòa followed me to the third floor and waited to see the library doors close behind me before going down to the student service office to finalize her paperwork. But Madame Hòa couldn't have imagined that Đỗ had already lodged himself inside, a few meters from the returns booth. And I couldn't believe it either. I was startled when I saw him."

Mrs. Huệ bowed her head in silence, and Mr. Đỗ picked up where she'd left off. He said that Mrs. Huệ was not the only one who was startled at the sight of him. He himself was startled when he looked in the mirror. His face was all hair. His clothes were disheveled. He had been lurking there for days. When the librarians demanded his student ID, there was nothing for it but to tell the truth. His particular mixture of French-Vietnamese-Lao baffled their ears, but they took pity on him and just gestured for him to sit silently in a discreet corner. During those few days when he had asked his boss for leave, got to the library at nine, planted himself behind this desk until six, and watched people work in deep silence, Đỗ had ample time to think. He had promised himself that this would be the last day he came to the library. He had three young kids, who all needed food and education. If he lost his job at the garage, the four of them would find themselves on the street the following month. The landlord wouldn't have the patience to wait for Đỗ to find another job. Neither would the four bellies of his children. In any case, he didn't know how to find another job. He couldn't allow himself to wait despairingly for Mrs. Huệ. In his circumstances, every such act was a luxury, and every luxury a peril.

He turned to look at Mrs. Huệ in silence. It was the first time he had turned to look at his wife during the whole evening. Perhaps it was the first time in over twenty years he had spoken out loud what he'd buried in his heart. And, strangely, it was also the first time he had paused for minutes on end without Mrs. Huệ picking up the thread.

I stood up and walked toward the window. Throughout the neighborhood, gates were closed and all seemed quiet. Only the faintest of lights could be seen on upper floors. It was hard to imagine that just a few steps away, the beef phở diner was serving its thousand customers a night, and next to it, the oil-drenched fried chicken rice shop was still displaying the hanging golden carcasses in its glass cabinet.

Across the road, a taxi screeched to a halt, the driver got out to open the rear door and dragged someone out, pushing them against the iron fence with one hand while ringing the doorbell with the other. All of a sudden the gates and yard were bathed in light, and a middle-aged woman in black bà ba pyjamas, likely a live-in help, ran to the gates. She handed the driver a bucket of water and a mop before reaching out with both hands to support the drunken passenger, who now illuminated was shown to possess a frizzy perm, Korean-style, dyed blonde, and a pair of pinkish legs peeping out here and there from inside her fishnet stockings. I had just recognized our neighbor when everything was again submerged in darkness. It all went so fast, and if any of the neighbors were enjoying the show from behind curtains, they didn't run out to offer any commentary. The gates of other houses remained mutely closed. The Sài Gòn rich can teach the West a thing or two about tact, it seems.

I came back to the sofa. My stomach was bubbling with hunger. The moment of intimacy seemed to have long passed, the couple only waited until I sat back down to continue. Mr. Đỗ was talking again. He talked about how he had stood up as soon as he saw Mrs. Huệ walk in that day in the library. He had told her that he was at the breaking point, and, gripping her shoulders, he asked her to choose right then and there whether to marry him or to return to her country. Embarrassed, Mrs. Huệ looked around at the librarians and other patrons. He told her that the fate of his family of four depended on her answer. Even more embarrassed, Mrs. Huệ noticed how the spectacle of two middle-aged people wrangling in the middle of the reading room had also aroused the students' curiosity, their faces turned down towards their books but their eyes stealthily glancing up. The harder he gripped her shoulders and urged her to speak, the more deeply she blushed and more stiffly she stood. Suddenly, there were the sounds of thumping steps. Madame Hòa stormed in. Towering over them both, she brushed Mr. Đỗ aside with one hand and pulled at Mrs. Huệ with the other. No one around had time to react before the library doors slammed shut and then the elevator doors a second later. Mr. Đỗ ran to the window of the reading room and looked down to the campus yard to see Madame Hòa walking casually before a skittering Mrs. Huệ, the latter hugging a plastic bag to her chest which bulged with all her unreturned books.

"I went home, my heart in shambles. I swore I would raise my kids on my own, and that women were all dead to me. Winters passed, summers followed, the days of hardship were left behind, my kids grew up, I grew old, all as it should be. It wasn't until 1990, my youngest son about to go to college, when I received unexpected word from Huệ. The letter's few short lines said that if I still wanted her, she was willing to be my wife. She was newly retired, and no longer feared accusations of debauchery and liaison with a Việt kiều. She had stayed in Hà Nội, in an apartment in the university block."

The housekeeper knocked on the door; dinner was ready. Mr. Đỗ and Mrs. Huệ hurried to stand up, hurried downstairs, their two tiny figures hurried to get lost in the immense corridor. I thought I would see them again in the dining room, so I was surprised to find the housekeeper alone in front of a small hill of nem. The two children were planted squarely before the TV screen. My brother Mai was out entertaining his guests in some five-star hotel. I sat down to dinner, and, while chewing, I thought about how my mother had time and again enthused about the good memories she'd made with her *colleague* during her fellowship, with never a word about Mrs. Huệ.

13 Sài Gòn

That night, for the first time, I imagined my mother walking on the boulevard Exelmans, the empty and dreary route connecting the Vietnamese Embassy and the Métro station, twice a day for three months, always with her two colleagues. The three women in that inaugural fellowship of the Ministry of Higher Studies constituted a unique trio, comparable to the French Three Musketeers or the Vietnamese Three Tank Crew Brothers: they ate at the same table, slept in the same room, traveled in the same Métro car, sat in the same classroom; where they went one, they went all. I imagined that during those three months they didn't once see the inside of a cinema, and saw the Louvre only from a passing bus, the National Library only from photographs, because Madame Hòa, the head of the group, maintained that capitalist culture was equivalent to imbecile depravity.

On a fine morning, a few days before their planned departure from France, the trio set out for a photo shoot with a camera borrowed from a friend. The Seine, the Eiffel, the Jardin du Luxembourg—they went to places that reeked the least of depraved capitalist culture. At the sight of Pont Alexandre III, Madame Hòa stopped, transfixed; she felt a rush of nostalgia, of the Great Russian land, where her five years as a student of French Studies were also her five consecutive years as Party committee secretary-*cum*-head of the Vietnamese students' association. She motioned to the other two to go stand in the middle of the bridge so that she could take their photo. The first shot, as even those least experienced with a camera would know, is experimental more often than not. The next two were of Madame Hòa, posing with my mother (taken by Mrs. Huệ) and then with Mrs. Huệ (taken by my mother). At the Jardin du Luxembourg, the sequence was repeated. First, Madame Hòa motioned to the other two to go sit on a bench in front of a rose bed and took their photo. But for the next two shots of her and either colleague, she wanted portraits, full body. She wanted to prove that her height, which earned her the moniker "the crane" behind her back, was a source of envy not only to the men in her life but also other women. Behold: on a path in the midst of blossoming roses, Madame Hòa was standing, arms folded, but my mother had had to climb onto the pavement, and Mrs. Huệ, most pathetic of all, had clambered upon a park bench.

The photo shoot pleased Madame Hòa to no end. In fact, the way she arranged the photos was optimally calculated, guaranteeing each would have two photos with either colleague, in every location. Perfect equality, perfectly ensured. Perhaps in this or that spot, they even had a passerby take their group photo: Madame Hòa would be in the middle, flanked by my mother and Mrs. Huệ. Those would be Madame Hòa's favorites (and a Party member wouldn't subscribe to the superstition against photos of three); standing in the middle could show off her height all the better. She would stare straight ahead, each hand on a shoulder of either of her scrawny colleagues. Like athletes on an Olympic podium receiving their medals. The central position highlighted her role as "leader of the group." Perhaps that's what Mrs. Huệ had meant when she described Madame Hòa as *the most imposing* fellow.

To summarize, at each location, each of them would have at least two photos of duos, and sometimes another of the trio. So should those taken with Madame Hòa be the only ones left in my mother's album, that probably means that she'd deliberately pruned the photos featuring Mrs. Huệ (the other possible interpretation, that my mother and Madame Hòa had gone out for a private photo shoot, is of course highly unlikely, seeing how the latter would never let Mrs. Huệ out of her sight, unless she was kept under lock and key in a secure room).

My mother's France photo album was put in a separate drawer. None of the photos had been framed and added to the jostling collection in the living room, which included her various selves receiving a certificate of merit, or bestowing an award, or sitting in a municipal meeting, or shaking hands with some ministers and vice ministers, or so on and so forth.

The story Mrs. Huệ and Mr. Đỗ had told me, though not explicitly featuring my mother, wasn't totally devoid of useful information. At the very least, I could now eliminate the possibility of my mother and Paul Polotsky meeting in Paris in 1977: under the eagle-eyed supervision of Madame Hòa, only an invisibility cloak could have helped her enter and then maintain a more than casual acquaintance (the kind of relationship involving a photo as keepsake) with someone outside the Embassy. So only the other theory still held: they'd met in 1954. The story also helped in corroborating Mr. Linh's account, that a Frenchman named Paul had been present at Hỏa Lò at the time my mother was imprisoned, and had watched her being led into an interrogation. That black-and-white photo had likely been given to her around that time, with he himself dictating what she had written on the back: *Paul Polotsky, 1954, 21 avenue de Suffren, Paris.*

If they couldn't have met for the first time in Paris in 1977, it was equally improbable that they'd reunited during that time. Let us suppose that on a rare occasion when Madame Hòa got a headache that sent her to bed early, or else was busy snooping on Mrs. Huệ, my mother had scribbled a hasty note to "21 avenue de Suffren" and furtively dropped it into the yellow mailbox in front of the Exelmans station. Suppose that Polotsky was still living at the same address as twenty-three years previously, and wrote a reply as soon as he got her message, to what address might that reply have gone?

My mother couldn't have let her guard down sufficiently to give him the address of the Vietnamese Embassy. She wouldn't dare even write it on the envelope as a sender's address: because if Paul Polotsky had moved, the letter reaching no receiver would have been returned to her at the Embassy.

And my mother didn't forget the example made of Mrs. Huệ and Mr. Đỗ. She was well aware that if her connection to Polotsky were exposed, her guilt would be twice or thrice as severe as Mrs. Huệ's: she was a married woman (while Mrs. Huệ was a bachelorette) and Paul Polotsky was a Frenchman (while Mr. Đỗ was merely a Việt kiều). And what could prevent Madame Hòa from investigating the origins of Paul Polotsky, and hitting the discovery of her life about how my mother had made his acquaintance during an imprisonment in Hỏa Lò. There would have been a veritable uproar at the Embassy. And an even bigger uproar back in Vietnam, in the Home Office's counterespionage agency.

My mother wouldn't dare contact Paul Polotsky by letter. If she ever happened to run into him on the street, she wouldn't dare say hello. Even if he was quick to recognize her, and came forward all beaming and stretching out his hand, she would've played the role of a stranger, shaking her head and saying, "What a pity, but I don't believe we know each other." And then, turning to Madame Hòa and shrugging: "These French! To them every Vietnamese looks the same!"

I suspect it was a role my mother could play quite smoothly, having taken the opportunity to practice whenever she found herself alone, in the bathroom or other private spaces where she would momentarily be free of Madame Hòa. Running into Paul Polotsky in the street might have been the nightmare that haunted her during that three-month fellowship. Was it the reason why, in all those photos of Parisian memories, she always seemed to cower before Madame Hòa, and her smile was always lopsided?

14 Paris

Paul Polotsky, huh? What I wanted was to smash his damn face in. But I didn't. Instead, I wrote him a letter. I don't remember exactly what I wrote. Must be the kind of soupy mushy corny banality that the dumbest chick can spew out in a heartbeat. But I knew the old bastard would gobble it up, hook, line, and sinker. And so he did. Two days after sending off that verbiage, I got a reply. He wrote that he was astonished I still remembered him after all those years, that in all those years he had lived in agony for forsaking me like that. He filled a whole darned page rambling about his *struggle between reason and passion*. And then another page yapping about the *sacrifice for his dearest fatherland*. He must've thought I was still that naïve stupid girl who'd been drunk on his empty bullshit; that he loved me, but the duty laid on him by the great organization prohibited him from leaving his wife who had stuck with him through thick and thin blah blah blah. And then he lamented about how lonely he was and would I please permit him to see me again. Of course, I said that I would. And he came right away, the old fool. He even seemed touched. His hands were trembling. Or maybe it was my imagination. Old people's hands tremble as a rule. But real or fake, I didn't care. I no longer wanted to discover who he truly was. I gave him some black tea with fresh lemon, I uttered some sweet reprimands. And I didn't forget to add certain seductive gestures to the mix. Afterward, I invited him to go for a walk. He jumped at the chance. I dropped some more sweet nonsense. And when the old moron was practically orgasming with delusion I jumped in a taxi, leaving the damn fool stranded in the bargain-hunting crowd. How I wish they'd trampled him to death. I would have sent a gigantic wreath to the funeral. But the bastard lives."

Listening to her no-holds-barred tirade, more than once I was astonished to think that this was the same woman who'd been on that promenade with Paul Polotsky, wearing her wide-brimmed hat.

A few days after following them around the town center of Montrouge, I went back on my own to the seven-story building with the gray gates and met the door lady, who gladly dumped the remainder of her sob story on me, then enthusiastically took me up to see *the Countess of Astrakhan* for my inquiry about *Monsieur Paul.* It turned out the door lady had recognized Polotsky the moment she saw him the other day, even though the last time she'd seen him was decades ago, during her own parents' reign as door lady and doorman. At that time, her mother had frequently charged her with small chores, such as bringing to the Countess of Astrakhan a cardboard box the milliner had delivered. Every time, without fail, the door would be standing open and, at the Countess's bidding, our good door lady would bring the box into their bedroom to witness with her own eyes Polotsky lounging on the bed with the Countess prostrate beside him, her arm around a cat, a so very romantic scene. "Monsieur Paul was so handsome and elegantly dressed, never seen without his sunglasses. The Countess, on the other hand, was no beauty, a mustachioed lady with an oversized nose, but she had a knack of dressing well, always looking like she was about to go to a party and, summer or winter, always with a hat on her head."

To my wide-eyed surprise she added, "In her apartment there is a room to display all her hats!"

My chance to confirm this came just a few minutes later. Even in the vestibule I could already see hat after hat, on little hooks dotting the wall. From the adjacent room a hoarse voice called out, instructing the door lady to take me to *the hat room*. My impression upon entering this room was that I had strayed into a hat shop. The collection must have held at least a hundred hats, filling wooden shelves high and low, most with a wide brim, some even with a gossamer-thin veil, but all with a tangible layer of dust. On the feather duster hanging nearby, the dust had turned white. In a corner, an exquisite marble fireplace also lay covered under dust, thick and silent. The whole apartment gave off a strange, tangy smell, a smell that was the sum of different smells, of perfume, hand-rolled cigarettes, dirty dishes, clothes begging to be washed, toilets screaming to be scrubbed, and another smell that I was unable to place.

My tête-à-tête with the Countess of Astrakhan lasted exactly ten minutes, as she had decreed on the phone when the door lady asked for an audience with her on my behalf, not because the high lady was occupied or looked down on the downstairs lady's "acquaintance," but because she was simply done with the topic of Paul Polotsky. After the tour around her hat room, I was led, not into her living room, but her bedroom.

The centerpiece of that room, measuring a few meters each side, was a massive iron bed on which pink satin sheets had lace trimming that looked to have been chewed by rats. Wrapped in a thin gauze nightgown, lounging half-propped up on a pile of dirty pillows, one arm around a cat, the other hand stubbing a cigarette onto an ashtray, the Countess of Astrakhan looked like the portrait of a prostitute whose youthful days were now behind her. Powder was caked on her furrowed face. The nose, though I'd grant not really "oversized" the way the door lady had described it, was a wrinkly blob in the middle of her face. Under the gauze, her breasts could be seen sagging nearly to her waist. But the most revolting feature had to be her hair, dyed black but still vanishingly thin so as to expose stretches of skin that a glance could tell you was soft as a worm. In haste I directed my eyes upward, to the literal portrait right above her bed, half-body, oil on canvas, in a golden oval frame. The woman in the portrait, the epitome of vulgarity, was no sight to behold, but still a million times prettier than the flabby mess reeking of cheap perfume that lay with a raised knee, casually showing off her thigh less than a meter from me. I couldn't link this human mass with the lady in the wide-brimmed hat, who had whispered so seductively to Polotsky before abruptly abandoning him the other day. Then I wondered, apart from the "Princess of Annam" and the "Countess of Astrakhan," how many representatives of exiled nobility were living in this seven-story building in this Southern banlieue. I once heard that my own block boasted a member of African royalty. And in a skyscraper in Chinatown a Laotian princess worked as a janitor, and in another a Burmese crown prince was plotting to return and take back his throne, very soon indeed . . .

The Countess of Astrakhan seemed very proud of the portrait. She had paid the artist, she solemnly announced, as much as a thousand francs, "which meant a whole month's rent"—and at that she put both hands on the cat to caress his back all affectionately. These days a hundred and fifty euros wouldn't get you a small basement storage. I imagined that the landlord or maybe his descendants had more than once been tempted to pay her a firearm-aided visit, only to be dissuaded by the specter of a life sentence, leaving her still alive and kicking in a cheap apartment surely the only one of its kind in Paris. She was, in the final analysis, a very farsighted woman. Even if she'd been a prostitute, she belonged to the shrewd variety of prostitutes. I tried to picture handsome Paul Polotsky lounging half-propped up on the dirty pile of pillows with her prostrate beside him, *a so very romantic scene* in the door lady's words. But my imagination refused to comply.

"Ever seen his sow?" the Countess of Astrakhan suddenly asked, her hands still moving ceaselessly over the cat. "What a perfect sphere, she rolls rather than walks."

I was startled. The woman I had always supposed to be Polotsky's wife was as gaunt as a stick and not even an inch shorter than him. I had seen them leave the house together at least twice, he going to the university, and she perhaps visiting a museum, a gallery, or an acquaintance, because she was always immaculately dressed, and her hair especially was done with such care.

"Perhaps he's got divorced in the meantime?"

My suggestion was met with a chuckle drawn out for a good half minute. I looked at my interlocutor, telling myself that at least she had a sense of humor. On the way here I had steeled myself for a full afternoon of a magnifique legend of love in lilac. But now the Countess of Astrakhan was laughing so hard her tears welled up, oozed in a black snake along her lower eyelids, and crawled all the way to the middle of her chin.

"How naïve can you be? Paul Polotsky will only go to a divorce court when hell freezes over. The chance is one in a million snowflakes in summer."

"Or perhaps his former wife had left him and now he lives with a new wife?"

"Never, that can never be," she replied hotly but with some hesitation, perhaps not absolutely convinced herself. But she calmed down instantly and, her spider-veined hands still caressing the cat with masterful skill (the cat was making moaning sounds), she looked right into my eyes and asked, her voice provocative:

"Know how high up the hierarchy he made it?"

Ah, that was something that had never crossed my mind. She was now helpless with laughter and signaled with a wave of her hand that I didn't have to answer. When her laughter subsided, she wiped her eyes with the sleeve of her nightgown and again leaned back against the pile of dirty pillows. The cat resumed his moans. I looked at my wristwatch and hurried to ask:

"In which organization did he serve?"

No sooner had the words come out of my mouth than the Countess of Astrakhan abruptly threw the cat to the farthest corner of the room, sat bolt upright, and pronounced:

"The topic of Paul Polotsky is once and for all banished to the trash can!"

Right on cue, the clock on the side table gave a shrill ring; the timer must have been set for "exactly ten minutes" as the countess had established with the door lady.

The cat recovered, looked around shaking and bewildered for a moment, then slowly walked out of the room. The Countess grabbed the half-finished cigarette, stuffed it between her lips, lit it, and exhaled a cloud of smoke from her nostrils.

I was then invited to stay for the black tea that she ordered the door lady to pour me from a samovar *long ready in the kitchen.* I looked at the three brown-stained glasses containing that pale liquid, wondering what Polotsky found in this old Baba Yaga. But now my concerns were focused on *in which organization did he serve.* And I wondered to what degree I could trust the various tales that had been dispatched from the Countess of Astrakhan's mouth.

15 Paris

It must be that whenever the Countess of Astrakhan was expecting a visitor, she would go out and scoop up some alley cat, bring it home, and give it some leftover canned food, muster all her skill into caressing it as a kind of show, only to send it flying the moment the audience was over. Certain cats, either too sentimental or too gluttonous, were determined to stay and enjoy her caresses and canned food, convinced this would be an end to a life of sleeping rough and constant hunger (for both food and love). Even after a kick in the butt or a defenestration, they still tried their best to return (by lying in wait in some corner of the corridor and weaseling in as soon as the door opened). If they happened to arrive at the lucky moment when she was expecting someone, they would be allowed to stay, to get some leftover canned food and some loving caresses, then a kick in the butt and a flight out of the window. Rinse and repeat. If, on the other hand, it was one of those unlucky weeks when she didn't have a single caller (the frequency of such weeks, unfortunately, only increased proportionally with her age), they would be starved to death, because the fuming Countess, taking her anger out on the hapless animals, would lock not only the kitchen door, so that they wouldn't be able to sneak in and help themselves to the days-old canned leftovers, but also the main door and all the windows, so that neither could they sneak out and find salvation in the public trash cans. No escape for the sentimental and gluttonous felines.

I took a sharp breath and told myself that the unidentifiable element in the tangy mix of smells was that of dead cats.

But why on earth did the Countess of Astrakhan feel the need to display her capability and desire to caress in front of me?

I put forth this probable theory: right after reading Paul Polotsky's reply, she'd gone out and found the nearest cat, on what may have been his last legs; the ancient cat was too weak to venture further afield, and had been nursing an empty belly since yesterday because the lids of public trash cans had been superglued shut by the naughty neighborhood youths.

She took the miserable elderly cat home, gave him all the rest of the canned sardines in tomato sauce left over from lunch, brought him to her bed, and began to caress him in earnest. It must have been ten years since she'd last performed the act; her hands were understandably awkward. But the result was extraordinary: the cat trembled with pleasure, and grateful tears rolled in a stream from his eyes; never before in his life of vagrancy had he had such a fulfilling and unusual meal, enjoyed such affectionate caresses. The Countess of Astrakhan looked at him in astonishment; never before in her life of wantonness had she met such a sentimental member of the feline folk. She decided to keep him until her reunion with Paul Polotsky. Her course of action was clear in her mind: two days later, she would give Polotsky the boot, as ruthlessly as he had done to her decades before.

Her plan worked perfectly. Paul Polotsky arrived a few minutes early, saw the open door but didn't dare enter until invited, and when inside her bedroom didn't dare sit down on the bed until invited, when offered black tea with fresh lemon didn't dare ask for sugar cubes, when sweetly reprimanded didn't dare offer justifications. All his eloquence regarding *the struggle between reason and passion* and *sacrifice for his dearest fatherland* had, in short, been used up in his reply, and the Paul Polotsky facing the Countess of Astrakhan now was only a fearful man apprehensive of his former lover's rebukes. Only when she drew the miserable elderly cat into her lap and stroked him with both hands did Polotsky's apprehension begin to ebb and his hope to timidly flow. The more the cat moaned with pleasure, the stronger the flow. A cat in her lap, he still recalled, was the medium through which she expressed her desire and exhibited her talent for caressing. As tears rolled in a stream from the cat's eyes, Polotsky's hope gradually strengthened into conviction. Then came the promenade in the center of Montrouge, she strutted in her long dress and wide-brimmed mahogany hat, as he followed close behind, at times bowing and whispering in her ears, the distant church spire, the lyricism of a nineteenth-century novel. All the sweet nonsense she let drop fanned his heart's gleeful flame. When he drew close to clasp her shoulders, he'd been fully convinced of her passion. But, as she herself had told me to so triumphantly, *when the old bastard was practically orgasming with delusion I jumped in a taxi, leaving the damn fool stranded in the bargain hunting crowd*. The decades-old score was thus settled.

Back home again, the first thing the Countess did was to give the cat a kick in the butt and a flight out of the window (right on schedule), then dusted off her hands, got into bed and took a long draw on her cigarette to savor her sweet victory. No one had ever been given the boot so ruthlessly as Paul Polotsky just now, she mused, imagining her shocked foe crumpling to the ground and suffering helplessly as pedestrians trampled on his thighs, his belly, his chest. "I should watch the papers closely for an obituary!" she purred mirthfully.

But after finishing her cigarette and reviewing the act, she began to lament the long idleness of her hands. She believed wholeheartedly in their potential greatness when it came to caressing; they simply needed frequent practice to avoid getting rusty. At that thought she jumped up from the bed, got out the thin gauze nightgown from her wardrobe and modeled it before the mirror.

Turning this way and that, she nodded admiringly: "Look how well I ward off old age!"

On a whim, she made a resolution: she would wage her war against all the fresh young girls. "Youth isn't everything, you'll see!" she said aloud, and sat down at her desk to scribble this personal ad: "Elizaveta the Countess of Astrakhan, of the dreamy green eyes, the wealth of experience and the spring of vitality, possesses such hands as are guaranteed to take you to heights no man has ever scaled. She welcomes all representatives of the stronger sex; age and color not a concern."

My ten-minute audience with her had simply been another practice session. Her reasoning went as follows: if women are also captivated by her caressing prowess, then even the most discerning male guests would easily be snared. Thus, right after the door lady's phone call, she had descended to the backyard to look for an alley cat and found the same elderly visitor from the other day. Despite his sentimentality, he was also a veteran with ample experience picked up through a life of vagrancy. After the kick in the butt and the defenestration, he had promised himself never again to try to sneak back in for some canned-food-and-caresses charity, the way dewy-eyed kittens did; advanced in years as he was, he would not tolerate such humiliation.

But the Countess of Astrakhan didn't give a damn about the elderly cat's firm resolution, she just hauled his ass upstairs and dumped out the half can of liver pâté left over from a few hours before. And then I walked in with the door lady, and everything happened just as I had witnessed it. Everything, except the cat's inner struggle! Yes, it's true, even if they wouldn't perform too well in any IQ test, cats do have such a thing as an inner life, and thus are likely to suffer at times from an inner struggle. Endowed with the half can of liver pâté and showered with caresses the moment guests appeared, the miserable elderly cat still tried his best to suppress his sentimentality. But when the Countess of Astrakhan mustered all her skill into caressing him with both hands (she seemed worked up when he didn't immediately tremble the way he had done the last time), the poor animal couldn't help giving himself over to a furtive dream about a snug-as-a-bug end to his days, under the wings of a generous and most lovely patroness.

But right at the moment he emitted the moans that seemed to cheer on the hands of the Countess of Astrakhan, who was at that moment the most loving benefactor he had ever known, she abruptly tossed him across the room and announced to me that *the topic of Paul Polotsky is once and for all banished to the trash can.*

Shaking, in bewilderment, the elderly cat slowly walked out of the room. He swore that he would get out of this place by any means necessary. While the humans were drinking black tea from their samovar, he did a quick tour of the apartment and soon realized that the main door and all the windows were tightly locked. But there remained one way out, and a pretty dangerous one at that: get into the fireplace in "the hat room," follow the chimney all the way up to the roof, and then, once outside, follow the gutter down to the ground. He was unsure that he could manage this challenging journey in his current state of health. He hesitated. He was advanced in years, but that didn't mean he was free from the fear of death. But he must have resolved to go eventually. I did two rounds of the apartment, but could find no trace of that elderly cat, so full of dignity.

16 Hà Nội

My father died ten years before my mother. By then they had been separated for ten years. They took each other to court when I'd finished primary school and my brother Mai had just graduated from college. I had never heard any explanation from either of them.

Under the French rule, my paternal grandmother had a shop that sold silk and fabric in Hàng Đào street. At one time, that shop had helped her feed her big family—her in-laws, her husband, and her five children; but later, the same shop had helped brand them all as "intellectual/petty-bourgeois elements," the *dregs of society* in the eyes of the new regime.

The only one who managed to remedy this stain on his Personal History was my father. The very day Hà Nội was liberated from the French, he quit school and joined the campaign to reform the private sector. After making lists and leading his comrades to knock on the doors of his mother's partners, he himself suggested his own family donate their two-story villa to the new government. "Suggested" was but a polite word for "pressured": his eldest brother was about to migrate to the South, and the family, afraid that they'd be reported to the local authorities, had no option but to go and live in the storehouse of a factory that the fleeing French owners abandoned.

My grandmother's two-story villa was assigned to a high-ranking government cadre.

My grandmother's partners' two-story villas were assigned to other high-ranking cadres.

His contributions recognized, my father was commended by the higher-ups. But he only gained their full trust after he wrote an announcement to publicly *disown* his eldest brother, who had by then arrived in Sài Gòn. My father was admitted to the Party, and appointed as one of the seminal cadres in Land Reform thanks to his experience in Private Sector Reform.

Unlike him, my mother's path to the Revolution had been smooth sailing from the start: her origin was among the "urban poor"; after getting her license to become a primary school teacher, she left home to join the Việt Minh, became a Party member at seventeen, and a liaison officer at nineteen.

At twenty, both my father and mother were granted exceptional permission to skip the first year of university.

At twenty-three, each graduated and was assigned a job at a prominent university in the city, where they taught and performed their duties as seminal cadres, first in the Youth Union, then in the Party.

My father's Personal History was perfect. So was my mother's. But they wanted them to be even better than perfect, and meticulously cultivated every single detail.

Reading my mother's Personal History, I would learn on which day/month/year she engaged in which duty, where it was and who was her supervisor, and all the honors and certificates of merit she accumulated.

Reading my father's Personal History, I would learn on which day/month/year he engaged in which duty, where it was and who was his supervisor, and all the honors and certificates of merit he accumulated.

Reading my father's Personal History, the section about his spouse, I would learn on which day/month/year my mother engaged in which duty, where it was and who was her supervisor, and all the honors and certificates of merit she accumulated. Reading my father's Personal History, the section about his siblings, I would never learn about that uncle in the South. Not until 1977, when that local policeman paid a visit to my mother, did I learn that my father had another elder brother in addition to his three siblings in the North, the eldest of them all, who had lived for twenty years "under the old regime in Sài Gòn." During his time in Hà Nội, my eldest uncle never visited my parents' apartment. And during that same time, my parents never visited the homes of their parents or their various siblings. With excellence, even with innovation, my parents fulfilled the role of the New Socialist Persons.

A few weeks before my brother took his university graduation exams, I witnessed a peculiar fight between my parents. The strangeness of the fight was that my father was the only one who raised his voice, and did so quite harshly, while my mother kept her head bowed in silence.

Standing in the middle of the living room, looking straight ahead at the window, my father, harshly: "You're a selfish woman!"

My mother kept her head bowed in silence.

My father, harshly: "You're irresponsible with your children!"

My mother kept her head bowed in silence.

I would never forget that narrow room, yellow in the light of the oil lamp, that early summer night so stiflingly hot, the tall figure of my father suddenly growing threatening, and the slender one of my mother for once vulnerable. Out the window, an unmoving blackness. I didn't know what my father was searching for out there. Not a dog barked. Not a leaf rustled. Even the insects were hushed.

I slept fitfully that night. Every time I woke up, I would part my mosquito net for a quick peep at the living room. There, my father was still looking straight ahead out the window, my mother still keeping her head bowed in silence. Every time, that same tableau. And every time, I would think to myself how it didn't suit my mother to play the role of the victim.

I was fully awake when dawn was nigh.

In the middle of the living room, looking straight ahead at the window, my father raised his voice: "Mai can't miss his fellowship in the USSR."

My mother kept her head bowed in silence.

My father continued: "Mai's Personal History has to be perfect."

My mother kept her head bowed in silence.

My father continued: "You must get a certificate of 'Unrelenting Courage in the Colonist Prison.'"

My mother kept her head bowed in silence. My father began to pace the living room, panting.

The whole apartment was filled with the sound of his panting, the panting of one about to be taken by Death.

He suddenly stopped in the middle of the room, held his breath, and pointed straight at my mother: "Woman, what did you do those three days in Hỏa Lò?"

To this day I remember how shocked I was to hear that question, or rather, to hear the voice in which my father asked it, a clear-cut voice I'd never heard from him before, a voice laden with suspicion, with outrage, with suffering.

I remember too that my mother was startled, almost imperceptibly, just enough for her shadow to tremble slightly on the wall opposite. But she maintained her silence. Her silence made me shiver in turn. I looked at him, then at her. The oil lamp in the corner was heaving its dying breaths. The heat was still thick enough to cut with a knife. My greatest wish at that moment was that my mother would relent and give an answer. I didn't understand my father's question, but I sensed the danger in it. The ten-year-old me, who'd just filled in my first ever Personal History form, had enough sense to deduce that if my mother didn't answer, that danger, that nebulous unknown in her history, would follow her for the rest of her life.

But my mother maintained her silence. Six months later, my parents divorced. My father was transferred to Sài Gòn, to his new post as a university vice director. My brother Mai went with him, and I stayed behind with my mother. Gone now were the days when my brother went shopping for groceries while I washed the dishes and swept the house, when my brother took me to school, when my brother attended my parent-teacher conferences, when my brother went to school and asked my teacher's permission for me to stay home because of the flu, or measles, or a sore throat...

Watching my father lug his suitcases out the door, I got the impression that it wasn't my mother he'd divorced so much as a danger, a nebulous unknown in the personal history. Later, I thought he must've had that question in his mind for the entire twenty years he'd lived with my mother, and that the fight that had lasted a whole power-cut summer night was only an excuse, a chance for him to cut his ties once he'd finished arranging in secret his vice directorship in Sài Gòn.

"Woman, what did you do those three days in Hỏa Lò?"

After the divorce, my parents lived separate lives. I never heard that question again. That question was what came into my head the moment I discovered the black-and-white photo of Paul Polotsky inside the cover of my mother's notebook, that evening in Sài Gòn, the day after her funeral. That question was forever associated with the image of her bowing her head in silence. Will I ever learn the answer?

17 Paris

July was finally here. Paul Polotsky had finished teaching a week earlier and now left home for the sole purpose of reading his newspaper in the park. Yesterday I had revised my tactics and decided to follow his wife instead. The meager information I'd gleaned about her thus far consisted of her name, Victoria (I had slipped inside the gates to read the nameplate on their mailbox) and her habit of dolling up (her clothes were always immaculate, and her lustrous hair always looked fresh from the salon).

I had, in fact, made up my mind to follow her right after my ten-minute audience with the Countess of Astrakhan (in which the old flame of the husband gave his wife the affectionate nickname *his sow*). But I knew it wouldn't be easy. In nearly a month of trailing Polotsky, I had caught glimpses of Victoria just a few times but already understood that the new target's comings and goings had no fixed pattern. Yesterday I'd waited until six o'clock, but she didn't even go near the gates. And after six I had to go pick up Mike from his day care.

Today seemed like it would be my day. I left Madame Wang's crafts shop and took the Métro straight to Polotsky's building. There, a little over an hour later, Victoria appeared at the gates, dress spick-and-span, hair flawless, red-nailed hands flaunting a veritable array of gems. But something in her appearance, perhaps her gauntness that even a stick would have envied, or her unsettlingly deep-set brown eyes, or her tightly pressed lips, told me that she was quite insufferable. I told myself that if I ever came face to face with her, I would first look up at her hair (she was a whole head taller than me) and then, when my neck became sore, down at her two beringed hands (a glance had been sufficient for me to suspect that these weren't market knockoffs).

Paris wasn't already scorching at six a.m. the way Sài Gòn and Hà Nội are, but by one p.m. the sky had become a steaming cast-iron wok. Victoria didn't take the Métro but the bus. I followed her, with my head a single misstep from butting into her back, and my heart from falling out of my chest. Fortunately, someone was quick to give up their window seat to her, so she spent the whole trip gazing out at the streets, oblivious to me watching her from behind. At first I hung back out of caution, but as the bus got ever fuller, I was shoved from all sides until I was close enough to see every shining strand of Victoria's hair. No need to crane my neck or stand on tiptoe, I had a clear view of the entire mane to admire for minutes on end. Mentally I compared it to the Countess of Astrakhan's hair, which had been dyed black, vanishingly thin, horrendously smelly. The exercise helped pull me away from the collective drowsiness in the bus, which for some reason was moving slower than a snail, the air inside a stagnant pond.

The trip would have been entirely uneventful if it weren't for the minor incident near the boulevard Courcelles. At the stop some few dozen meters from the Arc de Triomphe, where tourists filed off, the air inside the bus became a little less stifling and I somewhat more alert, I took the opportunity to move further back again, ending up beside a bona fide giantess, well over six feet tall and five hands in breadth, with a roughly three-year-old riding piggyback. The exhausted woman was standing still, all her energy being expended on simply breathing. By contrast, the skinny boy was hyperactive, turning this way and that and putting his hands everywhere he could reach. Thanks to his mother's exceptional height, he could carry out his hijinks without much difficulty. He touched the neck of the man in front, brushed the shoulder of the lady behind, grazed the ear of the child to the side, and pulled my hair several times, all in apparently high spirits, sometimes emitting a shrieking laugh. I didn't react. No passenger did. Everybody else in this ambulant oven seemed paralyzed. The memory must still have been fresh in them of last year's tragic heat waves, when dozens of thousands of lives had been extinguished in a single month of summer.

To fight off a new attack of drowsiness, I tried to imagine my brother's refreshingly cool living room, decorated to resemble Versailles, modelled by a French architect, and praised by the domestic papers as a great leap forward in Sài Gòn's interior arts scene. In the photos that accompanied the stories, my brother wearing a red cravat was seated on a gilded armchair à la Marie Antoinette, behind him a statue of Venus de Milo, and way in the back a copy of La Joconde. He oozed confidence. As may well be imagined, he has a lot of luck with the ladies.

The bus kept lurching forward. The passengers were silent. Even the hyperactive boy. Something seemed to have dampened his spirits. There was nothing much going on in the bus, nothing but the heat. At one point I happened to open my eyes just in time to see, right in front of me, the boy holding up a wig (like a new toy he had just discovered), and next to him a skull supporting a few wispy strands of black-dyed hair that belonged to Victoria. This scene, however, aroused in me only the faintest astonishment (I was no stranger neither to children's mischief nor to many elderly women's penchant for dolling themselves up).

What was truly shocking was what came next, when Victoria turned her head and pierced into the child's face with her gaze, brown-yellow irises emitting acid-green rays. It happened in a flash, and in complete silence: Victoria didn't shout, the other passengers didn't scream, and the mother didn't yell at her child. Without a word, the mother replaced the wig on the old woman's head. But I believed the boy's fledging soul was now marked with an indelible scar. He didn't burst out sobbing (if only he could have). His body was shaking in suppressed ripples and his face was a picture of terror. At three, he must have already seen a wolf, either in the zoo or in some animated movie. That night, he would probably have a nightmare. And from the next day on he would change drastically, avoiding people with blond hair at all costs, refusing trips to the zoo, turning his back on cartoons. But the nightmare full of wolf eyes would never release him from its grip, nor would he ever be able to confide in anyone. And in the beginning, his parents wouldn't be worried, they would be relieved: their hyperactive boy, an incessant nuisance to those around him, had become reserved and even averse to crowds. "He acts more mature than his age!" they would tell each other. Who knows what he would be like as a teenager, a young adult, a middle-aged man ... no one can ever be sure. But I couldn't help but recall *that dude Luc* from my Vietnamese class.

The bus pulled up at a major stop. The passengers flocked to the doors. I hurried to follow Victoria's descending footsteps. Released from the ambulant oven, finally. I could see from afar the round, glittering spire of the Russian church. The Cathédrale Saint-Alexandre-Nevsky, which, as all Parisians know, is located in the 8th arrondissement, on rue Daru, next to the boulevard Courcelles. At that moment, it dawned on me that back on the bus, while I was lost in a reverie of my brother's refreshingly cool living room, Victoria had been preparing to leave as soon as the bus stopped, but the moment she stood up the hyperactive boy grabbed her wig. Like me, he had been mesmerized by those shining blonde strands, desired to touch them but couldn't reach the seated woman from his mother's back, so had been forced to bide his time. He didn't cry and pester his mother to sit down, thus affording him some instant gratification. He could have done so, any other passenger would've given up their seat to a lady with such a young kid. Instead, he waited in silence. He didn't want to spook his target. And his chance had come soon enough, when Victoria began to straighten up in anticipation of moving to the door. So, while I had mistaken his calmer demeanor for dampened spirits, he was actually a very confident strategist. True, before those horrible yellow-irised eyes pierced into him, his mind was as perfectly developed as any three-year-old's. The problem is, adults tend to belittle three-year-old minds. I know I used to do the same, but Mike had swiftly rectified that. He was three when I took him to a toy shop on rue Tolbiac. After half an hour of deliberating, he picked a Transformer robot. The shop lady said, forty euros. I shook my head. After another half hour, he picked a similar robot half the size of the first one. The lady said, twenty euros. Again I shook my head, and Mike was about to pick another when the lady said, next time ask the price before you pick something, don't waste people's time. Mike said nothing. After that, every time we were to go to rue Tolbiac, he would ask me to check my purse, and if there was less than twenty euros, he would refuse to go. As he got older, he would do the checking himself. At three, having learned neither letters or numbers, Mike already knew that the more zeros at the end of a number, the better. At seven, having not long learned letters and numbers, I'd already witnessed the first currency revaluation, and I still remember how in the days leading up to it, the Hanoians brought out sacks to buy black market rice, because it was rumored that the price was going to double. Way after that, it was said that the Saigonese had heard the same rumor but didn't know what to buy, so on the day they brought out sacks of notes to burn …

In front of the church, a dozen people were deep in lively debate, seemingly on the topic of the China-Russia border and the four islands on the Amur. Victoria dove right in. Passionate argument. Impeccable clothes. Perfect hair. Ten blindingly red nails swimming in the air. Gem-studded rings glinting away. Every utterance beginning with *my dearest Paul says* … The audience couldn't help but admire. The little incident on the bus remained a secret.

18 Paris

The silver Mitsubishi was parked where the rue de Berri turns into rue d'Artois, in walking distance from the Champs-Élysées Plaza. Next to it was the driver sent by my brother's "business partner." Middle-aged, moderate height, well-groomed, with a balding forehead as polished as his faux leather shoes, which were deep mauve. Spotting me, he approached and introduced himself, he was from the Paris-Eiffel Real Estate venture capital company, entrusted with ferrying Mister Mai around during his stay. Then he immediately clarified that he was not a "taxi driver," but a "salaried employee" of the company. Then, scratching his head, he asked me to translate that to Mister Mai, "to avoid any possible misunderstanding." Behind the glass window, I had already glimpsed my brother, stretched out on the back seat, his cell phone lying forgotten on the floor, his Louis Vuitton briefcase crushed in a corner. The twelve-hour long haul hadn't been kind to his Sài Gòn flair, it seemed.

Yesterday, he had called me on my cell phone: "I'm flying over tonight. No need to meet me at the airport, I'll call you from the hotel. Tomorrow you'll be my interpreter." I hadn't slept a wink. I'd long suspected that my brother comes to France fairly frequently, but this was the first time he had contacted me on such a trip. I could clearly picture him sitting on the plane with the blanket drawn up to his neck, nodding in front of the small screen and at times switching to view the world map, on which the Pacific Ocean could fit in a palm, and a tiny zigzagging line connected tiny dots, each dot representing a city a million times bigger than itself. Phnom Penh. Bangkok. Yangon. Islamabad. Mumbai. Tehran. Istanbul. Sofia. Beograd. Wien. Strasbourg. The first and last, Sài Gòn and Paris, were marked by two tiny stars, flashing as they pleased. For the first time I was struck by how far away it is, Vietnam.

A glance at the agenda beside the steering wheel told me that we only had half an hour to get to the business partner's location, in a banlieue west of Paris. In the basement parking lot, on the way to the elevator, the driver said to no one in particular: "Ready to meet the big boss!" then looked at me from head to toe in disapproval: "Jeans are not proper." I said nothing. My brother asked, "What's the matter with you?" I told him, "I'm wearing jeans." He waved his hand dismissively. I know he doesn't like women in jeans either. His female employees all wear miniskirts.

It was hard to tell who the "big boss" was among the three gentlemen waiting at the door. Their appearances were different, to the point of night and day, but their demeanor was identical in its seriousness. Serious expressions, serious suits, serious speech. One by one, they shook my brother's hand, *hello Mister Mai*, and then mine, *bonjour Mademoiselle*. I wondered if every outsider who sees us supposes I am my brother's petite amie. I still remembered how, after that memorable dinner in Chợ Lớn the day after my mother's funeral, the long-haired waiter had produced a torrent of Chinese and my brother had blushed to his temples.

My brother pointed at the tall, fair-haired gentleman: "You are Morin?" The gentleman shook his head and indicated the man next to him, who was thin and dark-haired. My brother only nodded, and the other two didn't venture to introduce themselves. Maybe it was unnecessary.

Our entourage went up to the third floor, then down two short corridors set at a right angle to each other to arrive at a rather spacious meeting room. Inside, two rows of tables bore fresh flowers and bottles of Vittel soft drinks. On the right-hand row were seats reserved for my brother and me. Morin sat down at the central table opposite us. When everyone was settled, the tall gentleman went around distributing A4 dossiers, dozens of pages thick, on whose cover was printed, in a large bold font, "Résidence Eiffel Sài Gòn." When everyone had a copy in front of them, Morin addressed my brother: "Today we are here to review the contract, item by item, and if there's any disagreement, we will negotiate until we reach a final version."

I glanced over at my brother. I never would have imagined that he was here to finalize a business contract. The tall man began reading aloud. In the air-conditioned room I broke out in serious sweat. For a task like this, even Mr. Linh the former government interpreter would need a few hours poring over his dictionary, and someone of my level would need several days at least. On top of that, the tall gentleman read with a voice like a mosquito's buzz (at sharp contrast with his loud greeting), coupled with an unfortunate relish in linking sounds, so that even at the limits of my concentration sentence after sentence went through the sieve of my mind, sometimes leaving only the words "Eiffel" and "Sài Gòn." Around the halfway point of Article Three I had fully lost my thread. I grasped at individual words, translating those I caught and filling in the sentences by guessing at the rest. At times I simply made things up. At other times I just omitted things. It's likely that my voice, too, had sunk to the mosquito-buzzing level, and if that tall gentleman freely linked his words, I randomly swallowed mine. This must be how a nonswimmer feels when suddenly thrown into the sea.

My brother held up his hand as a sign for the tall gentleman and me to stop, then turned to Morin and asked in a loud voice: "Any difference from the version we went through the day before yesterday?" This, at least, was an easy enough translation. Morin shook his head. My brother continued, "So what are we waiting for? Let's sign it." The third gentleman, silent until now, stood up, introduced himself as a lawyer of the Paris-Eiffel company, and solemnly said, "According to the laws in this country, before signing any kind of document, the signatories have the right to read it however many times they please, until they understand it fully." My brother said, "I understand it all. You go ahead and read if there's anything you don't." At that, he took from his briefcase another A4 dossier of dozens of pages, on whose cover was printed, in a large bold font, "High-end Aparmens Eiffen Sai Gon," and beneath it the neat red stamp of the ITC-Vietnam Center for Translation and Notary Services.

Without breathing a word, Morin turned to the last page of his dossier and dashed a few strokes with his pen. A commoner's signature can never hold a candle to the flourishes of a "big boss"; his full name even unfurled at the end into a peacock's train. The tall gentleman hurried into position behind him, turning every page so that Morin could sign in the bottom margin. It all went surprisingly smoothly. After a few minutes, the dossier was handed to my brother. He also went through it at a sprint, in the opposite direction, twice as fast as his signature was half the size of Morin's, flaunting its dragon head beside the other's peacock plumes. Then he looked up and said he didn't need anyone to turn the pages for him, what he needed was a coffee, strong as hell, because it was now nearly midnight in Sài Gòn. The tall gentleman, after I translated, hurriedly dialled a number on his phone.

A female employee, in a questionably short dress the color of pink cotton candy, walked in and set a cup of coffee in front of my brother, then said in English: "If you need anything else, please let me know." He said nothing. Shrugging, the girl turned to me and asked me to translate into Vietnamese. I did, but he still said nothing. Shrugging again, the girl turned to Morin with a look of wonder. And when her "big boss" didn't react either, she shrugged a third time. Three shrugs in less than a minute. Her bared shoulders weren't so bad, but perhaps they were the only part in her body worth a peek. Her body, in that questionably short pink dress, couldn't fail to recall a ginormous leg of ham.

I recalled the serious expressions on the three gentlemen at the door, and figured that Morin must have anticipated a very tough negotiating session (it was, at any rate, the first time he had a partner from Vietnam), so he had devised a plan with a honey trap. Based on the way the female employee was dressed, the way she kept repeating "if you need anything else, please let me know," and the way she looked at her higher-up covertly asking for instruction, in all probability it was her to whom Morin had assigned that task.

I looked at Morin with pity and sympathy. If this leg of ham was the only honey available for his trap, he had failed spectacularly. It was baffling that a company about to sign a contract worth millions of euros couldn't shell out a fraction of that sum for some professional services. Then I wondered what was going through my brother's head, with all his female employees being either beauty queens or runners-up in various beauty contests in the North of Vietnam. But then again a thought crossed my mind: who knows, if a French bullfrog when in Vietnam might become a rhino, then maybe a Vietnamese rhino in France would become a bullfrog?

19 Paris

Half an hour later, the three of us were standing in front of a Russian restaurant, not by chance but on my recommendation: after wrapping up the signing, Morin had said that party A wanted to treat party B to dinner and would party B please suggest something they would like. I translated. My brother just shrugged. I turned to Morin, saying, "It would be nice to try some Russian restaurant." Morin seemed a little startled, looked from me to my brother, and finally said, "Russian restaurants, they are for watching, not for eating." My brother asked, "What's the problem?" I said, "We're having Soviet food tonight." My brother said, "Eating is overrated!" I said, "You've had enough of French cuisine." I wanted to add, "You've been in Paris so many times, and you never contacted me." But I kept this to myself. Morin glanced at us, then reached for his phone and ordered his secretary to book a table for three, "near the stage." The other two men excused themselves. Upon parting, my brother took from his briefcase two crocodile polos with Breton stripes, saying he had left in such a hurry, there hadn't been time to arrange some Sài Gòn gifts. The tall gentleman visibly brightened and let out a torrent of *thank you* and *merci* and *xièxie,* he must have thought Vietnamese and Chinese were one and the same. The lawyer forced a smile, probably still uncomfortable about the contract signing having proceeded Sài Gòn style.

"Little Russia" was located in one of the capital's poshest neighborhoods. The bilingual shop sign featured a shimmying young girl in a miniskirt, hugging a balalaika to her bosom. The restaurant owner couple came right to the door to shake our hands, gawping at me and my brother in bewilderment; this must be their first time receiving patrons of the Asian race, or a female customer in T-shirt and jeans. The two owners were plump and ruddy, the husband in suit and bow tie, the wife in a dress that came down to her heels, and whose neckline plunged to her cleavage. A certain rich, tasty smell wafted from them both. Hunger clawing at my stomach, I told myself that if Morin had anything against Russian food, I could clear his plates for him no problem. My brother's flair seemed to have been fully restored. He spoke a few words in Russian, the general gist of which was that he was very fond of the USSR, Lenin, Pushkin, the Red Square . . . The owner couple looked at one another. I translated into French. My brother and I both spoke the kind of Russian that a few years in a Hà Nội high school had given us, which actual Russians were entirely baffled by. My brother looked at me, smiling. The owner couple were also smiling broadly. Eagerly, the wife asked me to translate for the *dear comrade from Vietnam* that she and her husband were also greatly honored to welcome *you comrades* to their restaurant, that they too were very fond of Vietnam, Hotchimin, Hạ Long Bay, the beautiful Hà Nội . . . The husband added "Vietnamese food very good, Vietnamese women very sweet," winking at me as he spoke. I sighed; it really did seem as though every outsider assumed I'm my brother's bit on the side.

The restaurant interior consisted of an immense hall, almost unlit, perhaps to direct all eyes to the stage. Twenty or so tables were arranged in five rows. The owner couple had already vanished. Morin gingerly picked his way forward. Mai and I followed hand in hand. Our table for three was in the top row, right in the middle, facing the stage, which was splendidly decorated, mostly in red and white. Up on stage, a young man was playing the accordion and two young girls were singing a duet, a familiar melody whose name was on the tip of my tongue. Maybe Katyusha or Kalinka or something like that. I had to admit that all three were beautiful specimens, the young man tall and slender-hipped with the shoulders and chest of a bodybuilder and the face of an angel, his blond, wavy hair falling down to the side of his forehead, and the two girls who could have been twins with identical wide lamb's eyes, pinkish lips tracing a heart-stealing arc, and pinkish legs peeping out under identical miniskirts. A faint smell of butter permeated the room. I quickly sank into sleep, mindful of the small void in my belly.

I opened my eyes to realize that Mai and Morin had also drifted off at some point. On the table, the plates were still more than half-full. I chewed a small crêpe and looked up at the stage, where a muscular actor in Red Army uniform was reciting a Russian poem. Then I decided to get up. The reason I was here had perhaps nothing to do with eating nor sleeping. Slowly, I threaded between the rows of tables, on toes that felt like they were beginning to swell. The owner couple had split up, now he was at the door greeting customers, she at the bar commanding her delectable army of youthful waitresses, their miniskirts barely kissing their thighs. I had to wait quite a while at the entrance hall. The guests kept filing in. Contrary to what I had expected, Parisian Russian émigrés made up only a small part of the clientele, the majority were affluent foreigners and Russian tourists visiting from the motherland, whose money seemed to sing in their purses. Every single one was dressed as if for a ball, and with a satisfied look and confident bearing. Time and again a gentleman would take off his fedora and overcoat and hand them to me. I shook my head, should I be baffled or not, to be taken for a kept woman when by my brother's side, then, when on my own, a member of the waiting staff.

The owner was walking to and fro, the smile glued onto his lips. I approached him, and with all the courage I could muster said,

"Excuse me, do you know a man named Paul Polotsky?" Startled, he turned to me, and recognizing his rare Asian customer, he raised his brows, then shook his head: "Most regretfully, we don't know anyone by that name." My disappointment must have been evident on my face, because he asked in a tone of genuine concern: "Is it an important matter?" I nodded; he knitted his brows and said: "I have a friend who is the walking directory of the Russian community, but only with incredible luck can we get something out of him now. He is pushing a hundred and currently lives in a nursing home two hundred kilometers away. But one can never know! Give me your number."

I left my number with him and returned to my table. From a distance I thought I could hear a duet of snores. Mai and Morin—each hugging the back of a chair, heads lolling in opposite directions—looked like they were having a lively talk while asleep. Two empty vodka bottles were lying forlorn on the ground. On the stage, that famous ballet sequence, "The Death of the Swan," was now being performed, but the main dancer, with an angelic face and slightly too thick legs, didn't dance but rather wiggled her impressive butt, all but naked under the billowing tutu, resembling not so much a swan as a well-fed duck. The prince, for his part, was dressed as a gypsy, a brown pointy hat nearly covering his eyes. He didn't dance either, but made a few jumps on the stage, at times heartily slapping his partner's buttocks, who would then exchange lovey-dovey glances with him. A thunder of wild applause would rise up to reward such acts. Eventually, arms around each other's waists, the pair descended from the stage and went to bow at every table. The pointy hat now traveled belly up, so that the generous audience could put in their appreciation. The male dancer turned out to have a classically handsome face, blue blue eyes glimmering under the jet-black arcs of his brows. When the pair arrived at our table, Mai and Morin were still two snoring tractors. A loud whistle suddenly rang out somewhere in the room. Mai jolted awake, and perhaps was still woozy as he took out a crisp hundred euro note to drop into the hat. The actress bowed down and offered a hand to him. Mai, either confused or embarrassed, said *thank you* but did nothing else, and she left for the next table with a jerk of her bottom, which looked even more impressive up close.

Three bowls of salmon soup had been brought out just then, scalding hot and smelling mouthwateringly good. I thought I could eat for the three of us.

Five minutes later, leaving the restaurant, Morin shook my hand and expressed his regret that he could not see *mister and madame* off at the hotel. "My missus would complain if I was late," he explained in a worried voice. Glancing at Mai, Morin added, "Please take care of yourself tonight, ma'am. While you were out, your man emptied two bottles of vodka!" Mai looked at me and asked, "What's the matter with you?" Blushing, I said, "He said it turns out Vietnamese men are also ardent fans of the bottle." My brother shrugged, "You take a taxi and go home, I'm going to the Moulin Rouge!"

20 Paris

Back home that night, I discovered a fairly long letter in my mailbox. The sender was a certain Madame Lefebvre, and it was in response to a letter of mine six months earlier.

Six months earlier, after calling all the nine gentlemen named Polotsky scattered all around France, which had shed absolutely zero light on the current whereabouts of my quarry, I'd gone to the building at number 21 avenue de Suffren itself, where the doorman directed me to the managing company of the building, who directed me to their predecessor, who directed me to their predecessor, who directed me to their predecessor ... and, at the end of the line, it was the same perfect nothing waiting for me. In every place I was greeted by the same shake of the head: no, we've never heard of any Paul Polotsky. Having reached a dead end, I had to resort to writing a short note, which I then xeroxed into a dozen copies and dropped into every mailbox in the building's entrance hall, to ask if they *had ever known or heard of a gentleman named Paul Polotsky, who in 1954 had the fortune to live in this charming building.*

Every day during the following two weeks, I had lived in constant anticipation. But eventually, I'd given up hope. Madame Lefebvre's letter, arriving half a year after my note, was the first and only response it'd ever gotten. She let me know that, before taking up a pen to write this reply, she had wanted to first arrive at a *relatively accurate answer* (that phrase was underlined) and that answer was a resounding no: both her mother (having since relocated to a city in the southernmost corner of France) and her grandmother (in a nursing home for the last ten years), who had lived together since the very beginning of the Second World War in the same apartment where Madame Lefebvre was living now, had confirmed that they *had never known nor heard of a gentleman named Paul Polotsky* (she deliberately echoed the words in my note). But, again, she must emphasize that this answer was only *relatively accurate,* because, in her experience, *on the contrary to what many still assume to be the truth, there are inherent limits to human memory,* and *life indeed harbors a wealth of hidden possibilities that our imagination is woefully inadequate to explore in any exhaustive manner.*

She proposed three hypotheses, as follows:

One: Paul Polotsky had lived in this building for only a few months, and during that summer. "You know, no one ever stays in Paris in July and August, and even if certain people are there in body, their minds have already packed their bags and gone on a vacation."

Two: Paul Polotsky had lived in this building for more than a few months, and not in summer, but he was a virtual recluse. "You know, there are people who simply don't have that need to go out and socialize, even to go stand on the balcony to engage in people-watching, and those are often the very people who whine the loudest about their solitude."

Three: Paul Polotsky had lived in this building for quite a while, and was not that terminal a recluse (that is to say, if he bumped on someone on the stairs or in the hallway, he was perfectly capable of nodding his head and mumbling "how do you do?"), but her mother and grandmother had totally forgotten him, the way people frequently do forget things. "You know, it's an oft-observed phenomenon to open a notebook from a few years ago only to find names that no longer ring any bells or evoke any faces, no matter how much you rack your brain."

Her final conclusion: "There are cracks in our memory that at first sight seem negligible and harmless, but leave them untended for long and before we know it, they yawn open into abysses that devour all we once swore would be forever cherished in our mind."

I finished the letter and thought, there is another, very obvious hypothesis that Madame Lefebvre somehow didn't pose: Paul Polotsky had never lived at number 21 avenue de Suffren.

21 Paris

I stood in front of a full-body mirror in the changing room, beside me a pile of clothes with their tags still on, not the clothes of my own choosing.

That morning, after dropping Mike off at his kindergarten, I had gone straight to the Champs-Élysées Plaza Hotel, where the driver from Paris-Eiffel company whisked my brother and me to the Galeries Lafayette. On the women's floor, my brother told me: "I'm going out for a smoke. There's almost ten thousand on the card. Call me when you're done." I was taken aback. I'd thought he'd come here to buy presents for his connections back in Sài Gòn. Before I'd had time to say a word in response, he was already gone down the elevator. I didn't know what to do. I put his Visa card in my handbag, and it was like a sudden weight pulling at my arm. It was the first time I'd ever had that kind of money at my disposal. Presently, a shop assistant came over and asked what I was looking for, miniskirt? maxi skirt? suit trousers? blouse? cardigan? . . . She kept bombarding me with questions, and I was at a loss for words. I'd barely paid any attention to my clothes since parting from Kai. One day I just opened my wardrobe, picked out everything I'd ever worn to go out with him, filled two cardboard boxes and brought them down to the basement storeroom, only keeping a few basic items to wear. Sometimes I thought, even if Kai bumped into me now in the street, most likely he wouldn't even recognize me.

Standing in front of the mirror, beside the pile of clothes the shop assistant had picked for me, I didn't know what to try on first. I removed my own clothes piece by piece, thinking of how Kai had once delighted in removing them. Every time we met in that small attic, he would make me sit very still while he unfastened my blouse, button by button, finishing with the tiny ones on my cuffs, then unzip my skirt, then remove my belt. It felt like the longer he could unwrap me, the more excited he got. He did it in a half-solemn, half-innocuous way. He even, once, asked to see my vulva, and he looked at it with such fascination, parting hairs strand by strand, the way a curious child goes exploring.

We used to make love on the wooden floor. His arms wrapped around my back, every gesture deliberate, revealing to me another side of him I hadn't known. It is often said that intercourse is when the human lets loose the animal within. But with Kai it was somehow different. The first time he entered me, I was nothing but a bundle of nerves. The only thought in my head was that perhaps I wasn't attractive enough for him. Impatient for it to be over, I suddenly squirmed after just a few seconds, and he ejaculated. We got dressed in silence. But with each time I got more and more aroused. I came to understand that, with Kai, what he unleashed during lovemaking was no hidden animal, but the human he aspired to be. The everyday Kai was constantly irritated; Kai the lover was infinitely calm. The everyday Kai was curt and always pressed for time; Kai the lover was tender and patient as a saint. With each time, I grew further convinced that my own desire to make love to him stemmed from my wish to discover the human he aspired to be, the dream he hid deep inside himself, a dream known only to the two of us. So instead of playing the womanly role and closing or half closing my eyes, I tried to open them wide to gaze into his face, fascinated by the wondrous modulations that played out there. And he did the same, always opening his eyes wide to gaze into my face, fascinated by the wondrous modulations that played out there, desiring to explore his own hidden dream.

* *

We made love on the wooden floor, in silence. The attic room was hot as an oven, absorbing every ounce of the summer heat. He always arrived first, opened the door and window, poured a bucket of cold water over the floor, and covered the window with a piece of red cloth he'd found at a nearby grocer's. The room was bathed in red. An unspeakable yearning filled my being. He often lay on top of me, his hands wrapped behind my back, his legs stretched out on the floor, then thrust lightly inside me, pushing me gently to every corner of the room. And I relaxed my body and stretched out my legs, my hands on his shoulders, my eyes always wide-open, gazing into his face. Looking back now, I imagine my own face must likewise have been a portrait of solemnity. Kai and I, our faces were never once distorted by pleasure or lost in ecstasy the way it's usually described. Kai and I, two solemn faces facing each other, two pairs of eyes wide open, gazing together into his deepest hidden dream.

The last time we made love, after it was over, we made a quick visit to a gallery on the top floor of an abandoned factory. In front of a large Kandinsky painting of the artist's childhood home, seen from above, in the dreary autumn light, Kai whispered in my ear an endless whisper of which I only caught the last words: "... whatever happens I'll never forget you." I didn't understand a thing; I wanted to ask him about Kyoto, about his childhood, about things he'd never told me and I'd never dared ask ... No specter of separation disturbed my mind. I smiled and turned my back to run. In the Métro I took a short nap, and when I woke back up the car was empty, and there was an announcement on the loudspeaker that the train was pulling into the depot. I always need a short nap after an afternoon of love. But I never told Kai this. He and I, as a rule, never said such things to one another, as if, voiced, the dream would be secret no more. Perhaps that's why we never seemed like a couple outside of the attic. And he would soon become irritated again.

I took out my phone. I wanted to call Kai, to tell him that I loved him, to hear his irritated voice that had been missing from my life for so long. But with my phone already in my hand, I realized that I no longer remembered his number, not one of the eight digits that followed the initial 6. Panicking, I fumbled through my notebook and found his number written in his own hand, the day we first met, on the bus, when I was on my way to pick up Mike, and when Kai was coming back from the airport. The second I saw those numbers, in his neat and steady handwriting, my fingers began trembling like mad, and I had to dial the same numbers again and again. The phone rang once. Twice. On the third ring, the premonition in my fingers was confirmed: the operator's voice came on the line to tell me *this number is no longer valid.*

I stood there still, naked in front of the mirror, beside me a pile of clothes with their tags still on. After I don't know for how long, I was startled when the shop assistant called from outside the changing room, asking if I had found anything to my liking. I couldn't answer, tears were streaming into my mouth, and I kept swallowing big gulps of them. My tears smelled like Chanel N°5, because when my brother and I passed the perfume booth next to the clothes store, the perfume lady had pulled me to her, sprayed me from hair to bosom, then declared in the kind of Vietnamese they speak in Chợ Lớn: "You should buy number five, love, it's really something!" Then to my brother she said: "Your Hà Nội wife is such a cutie!" I glanced at him, who was vehemently shaking his head.

I stood there still, naked in front of the mirror, the phone in my hand making weak beeping sounds. After I didn't know how long, I was startled when my brother called from outside the changing room: "What's the matter with you? I kept calling but your phone was always busy!" I couldn't answer, my mouth was still full of tears even though I had been drinking them down in gulps. I hurried to put my own clothes back on and left the changing room, carrying the pile of clothes with their tags still on, not one of which had been tried on. My brother asked again: "What's the matter with you?" I swallowed the last mouthful of tears and said, "Something is wrong with my phone." My brother waved his hand dismissively. He took the pile of clothes from my arms, handed them to the shop assistant, and gestured to her to ring them all up.

22 Paris

Half an hour later, the two of us stood in front of an old apartment building on a street that bordered the 19th arrondissement and the northeastern banlieue. The small lane circumventing the building was littered with trash, and cigarette butts dotted the wild shrubs as a kind of weirdly spiky flower. The recent rain had left a conspicuous puddle to the left of the doorway, where green bottle flies were having a party on a bounty of banana and pineapple skins. A congregation of youths, hands in pockets, saliva hissing in their mouths, leeringly assessed the newcomers. My brother took a piece of paper from his chest pocket and entered the code into the door keypad. We stepped inside the building, followed by a few obscenities from the youths, including a loud "Happy fucking!" In the pitch-dark hallway I dared not turn to look at Mai. At the end of the hall was a small yard stinking faintly of sewage. I had the feeling that, from behind those long-unwashed curtains, a few dozen eyes were fixed on the two of us, in a way that had never happened for me and Kai. On the ground floor, the door to the apartment on the right stood ajar. Mai pushed it open and walked in, gesturing for me to follow. It was a rather large apartment, with at least four or five rooms, but every door was closed, and the only audible sound was the faint whirring of a VCR. My brother paused, listened, then went to knock lightly on the last door on the left. No answer. After half a minute he knocked again, harder this time. The sound of the VCR abruptly cut out, followed by that of a chair scraping back and footsteps hurrying to the door.

The door opened and a man's face peered out. The elderly, but ruddy and well-preserved man uttered a single acute cry as if to convey his astonishment. My brother smiled, glanced at me, and turned to our host, whose full body was now visible in his attire of suit, tie, and gold-rimmed glasses, very elegant and in glaring contrast with his surroundings. Regaining his composure, he ushered us inside with arms wide open. My brother walked in, and I followed him, racking my brain to recall where I had seen this face before.

We were led to a dark violet faux-leather couch. The older man sat down on a matching armchair, behind a faux-wood coffee table which bore a set of six teacups and a few copies of *Playboy*. He glanced at my direction as if wanting to say something, but thought better of it. Then all three of us fell into silence, each pursuing a private train of thought. Mai, motionless on the couch, looked deep in somber thoughts.

My parched throat soon began to bother me. To distract myself, I imagined that the six cups in front of me were brimming with vối tea. Then, to forget that tangy, pleasant-smelling brew I hadn't tasted in years, I invented a business deal, Sài Gòn–style: this man had visited my brother's office to ask for help renting a five-star villa near the Independence Palace, and, while he was there, advised Mai to invest in real estate in the City of Light: "There are plots over there that are even cheaper than in Sài Gòn!" Mai was startled. He'd been led to believe that a single square meter in Paris would set him back fifteen thousand euros, as this was the price advertised on the billboards near the Parisian hotels he always stayed in. The two men immediately outlined a joint investment scheme: within six months, the older man would provide a list of five parcels of real estate, zoned for development and complete with the necessary building permits, and Mai would shell out at least five million euros in capital. The building we were now sitting in was on that list. And my brother's somber thought was regarding the best way to erect a brand-new, state-of-the-art, five-star résidence, the first of its kind in one of the least fancy districts in the French capital.

Suddenly we could hear noises coming from the other side of the wall, unmistakably the squeaking of a bed frame. Mai found the remote control and pointed it at the TV. Our host half stood up to stop him, but it was too late. The TV screen blinked on, showing a couple engaged in vigorous exercise: the male actor, naked except for his briefs, his bodybuilder's muscles on full display, was carrying his supine partner, a woman dressed in a way that refused to acknowledge she was no longer in her youth, with her hair swept way up into a high ponytail at the crown of her head and adorned with a gigantic pink bow. While Mai was fumbling with the remote to turn the TV off again, the male actor kept shoving her head against the wall, while she, eyes shut tight, mouth agape, was panting so hard the pink bow was shaking mightily, and kneading the breasts that threatened to burst out of her perilously buttoned white blouse that could have been a high schooler's but for its sheerness. The screen went dead. The panting didn't, but grew somehow more urgent. It was coming not from the screen but from the other side of the wall. Undoubtedly, the athletic activity shown on the TV screen corresponded to the heavy thumping of the bed frame next door.

The older man shook his head and looked at us, holding up his hands in a show of resignation, then blurted out: "Crazy, the bunch of them!" I looked at his face, transfixed. Alas, I finally recognized our former neighbor Điền, once the prolific subject of earth-shattering rumors in our block. He was now quite another person. Once skinny and dark, he was now vibrant and ruddy. Once wearing his all-season uniform of robin's egg blue shirt and soldier's pants, he was now dressed as a man of means. Once a proper man who only read the Party's *The People*, he was now a consumer of porn and *Playboy*.

A child of his native Hà Tây, Mr. Điền could never pronounce the falling tone; even his own name came out of his mouth as "điên," so behind his back everyone had called him "Điền điên," crazy Điền, even though he was probably the least crazy person I had ever met. Mr. Điền had been a food engineer back in the day, and twenty years ago he'd gotten a slot to go to Cuba to study cane sugar production, but when he landed at Charles de Gaulle he'd thrown away the Havana-bound ticket and stayed in Paris to build his career—he had become a *loose bike chain*, in the parlance of the time. If I could recognize him today, it was solely thanks to the dialect unique to Hà Nội's rural little sister.

The panting finally stopped. Mr. Điền became much livelier. He invited us out for lunch, but told us we would have to wait a while first. He explained that he was the owner of this apartment, and had split it into smaller rooms to rent; he was expecting new tenants today, whose contract signing would take around thirty minutes, after which "wherever in Paris you want a peep at, whatever delicacies you want a bite of, you kids' word is my command."

At that point, someone knocked on the door. A young couple walked in, their arms around one another. Students from Hà Nội, here on a parental scholarship. Mai took my hand and led me outside. Before leaving, he gave Mr. Điền an address and told him to meet us there an hour later. The older man took out a fifty-euro note from his wallet: "You kids take a taxi!" Mai smiled. I shook my head, Mr. Điền must have no clue as to my brother's rank in the Sài Gòn real estate scene. Then I told myself I'd been way off the mark imagining a joint investment scheme, such a thing could never happen between Mr. Điền and Mai: the former leasing cheap rooms to students, the latter turning his own mother's funeral into an opportunity to sell hundreds of luxury condos.

The youths shrieked with laughter upon seeing us leave the building, and the loudmouth from before feigned surprise: "How fast these fuckers fuck!" I again blushed to the roots of my hair. Mai looked at me, "What's the matter with you?" I said, "He was asking for money." Mai waved his hand dismissively. On the way back, the driver complained that this was the most terrifying neighborhood around, drowsy as he'd been he didn't dare leave his car to go for a hot coffee, otherwise he surely would have returned to a broken window or missing headlight.

The car crawled forward. A protest had practically shut down the street. Nurses from public hospitals were demanding higher wages and shorter night shifts. Mai was motionless in the front seat. I assumed he was again pursuing his own train of thought. His somber look in Mr. Điền's living room was still bugging me. Only when a policeman tapped on the window and asked us to turn onto a side street did I understand that my brother was fast asleep. I had to comfort myself with the thought that it wasn't yet midnight in Sài Gòn.

When we arrived and the driver was looking for a parking space, I looked at my phone. I had a new message: the owner of "Little Russia" had managed to contact *the Russian community's walking directory*, the one who was pushing a hundred but whose memory was still sharp as a blade; this man had confirmed that he had once met a man called Paul Polotsky, a bachelor, a high school teacher in a Parisian banlieue, passionate about playwriting, who had died in a traffic accident in the 1960s; the owner would call me again if there was any further news.

23 Paris

A floating restaurant on the Seine. It was already past two p.m. and only a few guests were left. Mai had chosen a table outside, close to the water. The table was beginning to fill up with food when Mr. Điền walked in. Under natural light his face still looked ruddy, but now his numerous wrinkles were showing. However, his talent for camouflage had really come to his rescue. If those gold-rimmed glasses hadn't held transition lenses, I bet whole crowds of crow's feet would have been visible at the corners of his eyes.

Mr. Điền sat down and categorically dismissed his knife and fork. He asked only for a glass of beer on the rocks, but didn't touch it after the waiter brought it to him. His vacant gaze was lost in the distance, as he was lost in thought, until he asked Mai, "Did you meet little Liên?" His voice held the hint of a tremor. My brother responded, "Why don't you come home for a visit?" Still looking into the distance, Mr. Điền said, "I've applied for a visa but it hasn't been approved." Mai silently took a color photograph from his coat pocket and showed it to Mr. Điền. The old man fumbled to put on his presbyopic glasses, and hastily took the photo. In it, a woman, still young, quite a beauty, and fashionably dressed, was standing in front of a blue sea, whether real or a backdrop it was hard to say.

Mr. Điền turned the photo this way and that in his hands, nearly dropping it more than once. Suddenly he asked, "Did you meet my … her?" My brother said, "She sends her regards." Mr.

Điền's face, blushed just now, visibly paled. Motionless, speechless, he sat. The three of us stayed silent, with the burbling sound of water below us, a tabletop covered with food in front of us, and the sunlight now beating down above.

Thinking back, I figured that all those years ago, his wife and daughter wouldn't have known any sooner than their neighbors about his decision to stay in France. It was likely that the local police had paid his wife a visit; the same policeman who'd informed my mother about the existence of my eldest uncle a few years previously would have knocked at their door, sat down, looked around the room, then sternly asked his wife, "Have you received any news from Mr. Điền?" His wife had heard no news, but she had immediately intuited that something unsavory was going on, so she didn't know what to say. The policeman continued: "Anything suspicious in his behavior before he left?" She shook her head; he had gone to Hà Tây to visit his parents and younger siblings, which was something he did before every long work trip. The policeman went on further: "Does he have any relatives in France?" She shook her head again; she had had no reason to question what he'd listed in his Personal History. Before standing up to leave, the policeman looked her straight in the eyes and said, "Any time you get news from Mr. Điền, you're obliged to report to us right away!" Leaving the poor woman to her fright, he then paid a visit to the head of the local civil unit, asked the same questions, received the same lack of enlightening answers, so before leaving he looked the local head straight in the eyes and said, "Any time you get news about anything suspicious in Mr. Điền's wife and daughter's behavior, you're obliged to report to us right away!" While the local policeman, now back at his office, was calling the Police Department to make his report and ask for advice, the whole block was in a frenzy with the news that Mr. Điền had become a *loose bike chain*. It was hard to say who was the very first to use the phrase, but immediately they became the buzziest words in the whole block. They could be heard everywhere, around the public water tap, on the stairs, in the yard, at the gates, in the corridors, in the long winding lines for rationed bread or for the collective toilet in the yard . . .

The rumor had started succinctly enough: on Mr. Điền's way to Cuba, the chain had got loose in France. A few hours later, the talk had sprouted new details: on his way to Cuba, the chain had got loose at his relative's house in France. A day gone by, and a whole intrigue had developed: Mr. Điền's relative in France had served in the French army before 1954 (hence said relative's absence from his Personal History), and now, demobilized, was the owner of several Vietnamese restaurants in Paris; they needed a food engineer who could conjure up Northern Vietnamese delicacies like tofu, fermented bean paste, stinky shrimp paste, full-fetus duck egg, or the infamous dog meat, using only Western European ingredients; they had contacted Mr. Điền and invited him to France; they had assured him that all he had to do was to find a way to CDG airport and they would take care of the rest; they had promised to pay him the same as French food engineers; and now everyone understood why, while his colleagues at the Hà Nội Food Industries Research Institute fought a battle royale for a slot to go to the USSR, the GDR, or Czechoslovakia, the unassuming Mr. Điền had applied for a short-term trip to Cuba; he had discovered through diligent research that the Moskva–La Havana airplane was likely to touch down at Paris to replenish its stock of fuel and baguettes, a circumstance most favorable to his chain-loosening plan . . .

From that day on, his wife and daughter, little Liên, dared not step out of their home. It was a time when envy could be ignited over who got the less moldy rice using the same ration book, or who could afford morning glory at market price on the same civil servant salary as those who had to be content with government-store greens. So Mr. Điền's chain-loosening fortune in France, the warm welcome he was supposed to receive and the cushy wage he was supposed to enjoy, cost the whole block many sleepless nights. No one was clearheaded enough to verify the trustworthiness of those rumors, and for all we know, at the very moment his old acquaintances were whipping themselves up over his incredible luck, Mr. Điền could very well have been sleeping under a bridge or in a dingy street corner, since as an undocumented person he didn't dare go to popular areas to ask for some job as a porter or window cleaner, and as a Party member, a cadre from the socialist North, he didn't dare avail himself of the hospitality of the Việt kiều community for a dishwashing or kitchen hand position. And the embassy, of course, had to be avoided at all costs. He got a few francs from some passing good samaritans, and was burning to send a wire home, but a few nights' deliberation told him that the time had not yet come.

His wife and daughter, little Liên, dared not step out of their home. After a few days cooling her heels, his wife was summoned by her supervisor to submit a mea culpa and receive in turn the decision to terminate her job. After a few days cooling her heels, little Liên was summoned by the school staff to submit a mea culpa and receive in turn the decision to move her to the class for the worst-behaved. The head of the local civil unit and the local policeman took turns writing reports on them. Where they went at what time, what they did, whom they met, whether their blouses were patterned or plain. They were all recorded down to the last detail.

After a short while, the block's tiny realm was shaken by yet another earthquake: an acquaintance of an acquaintance of an acquaintance of someone had recently gone to Paris and bumped into Mr. Điền, who'd been seen linking arms intimately and so publicly with a Việt kiều woman; he had "gone Western"—been naturalized—and even changed his name; he looked younger now, more energetic, and was dressed to the nines. This new earthquake had the unexpected effect of drastically cooling their collective envy: it gave way to collective pity, and people lined up at the Điền apartment to offer their condolences to the wife and daughter. A few days later, his wife was summoned to her former office and advised to resume her post, and little Liên was summoned to the school staff room and told to return to her former class.

One afternoon, home from school, through the wide-open door of Mr. Điền's apartment, I saw the family who had just moved in laboriously throwing out all the things his wife had deliberately left behind, most of which were his books, including an old Đào Đăng Vỹ's *French–Vietnamese Dictionary*, which someone swiped right away and sold to a scrap collector (at that time, Hanoians hadn't yet caught the dream-fellowship-in-France fever, so a dictionary whether old or new could only fetch a few dozen đồng, enough to buy two bowls of phở at the government stores).

That same evening I heard, out in the corridor, the newcomers telling our neighbors that a widowed colleague of Mr. Điền's wife had taken pity on the plight of the mother and daughter and taken both home to care for them. But their cohabitation had no chance of being officialized: Mr. Điền's wife was, legally, still married to Mr. Điền.

The saga of Mr. Điền began to fade from the block's lore. The collective envy could always find new targets, no less extravagant: a homely woman, fated to be alone forever, who suddenly bagged a Swedish expert here to redesign the citywide water-tap system; a man who visited the flea market on Huỳnh Thúc Kháng street during a work trip to Sài Gòn, picked up an old nonworking transistor radio for less than a bowl of phở, took a hammer to it to try and fix it and was flabbergasted to discover a pack of dollars as green as the day they were printed; but the most renowned figure had to be a jobless man, one of the poorest in the block, who bribed his way into a manual laborer's job in Siberia, then became so successful in his wheeling and dealing he was granted the title of *marshal* by fellow businessmen, and every month he sent back home a huge shipping container filled with refrigerator after refrigerator, which were filled with pressure cooker after pressure cooker, which were filled with wheel bearings, gold rings, and antibiotics, so the family kept opening layer after layer without seeing the end of those beautiful Matryoshkas.

Mr. Điền picked up his glass of beer, though the ice had all melted and the foam dissipated. His hands were clumsy. His nails were carefully manicured, but green veins showed thick as fat worms. He made to take a sip but then abandoned the attempt, looked up and asked, "How's Liên?" Mai said, "She gave me your address." Mr. Điền said, "Every time I send money home, she sends it back." Mai said, "She does the same with the money I send her." Mr. Điền was silent. As were we.

When daylight had all but faded, Mr. Điền stood up and said he needed to go. He took out two name cards, gave one to Mai and said, "Tell Liên that I'm still well," and the other to me, "Let's go find an old friend of your mother when you have time." When he had left, my brother said to me, "What's the matter with you?" I said, "He doesn't know that mother is dead." Mai shook his head. I put the card into my handbag. On the card was written in English and French, *Didier TRAN, investment advisor.*

24 Paris

What's the matter with you?"
"Nothing."
"Come back to Sài Gòn. Live with me."
"It's very kind of you."
"A woman shouldn't live alone like you do."
"I'm used to it."
"I've built over a hundred luxury apartments. Take your pick."
"I prefer it where I am."

In the Ritazza Café in the airport, the noise had died down. Mai had finished his spaghetti plate and was waiting for his coffee. The clock on the wall read three p.m. Another half hour before those flying to Seoul must be present at the boarding gate. I looked at my brother, acutely aware of the lump in my throat:

"Do you know why our parents split?"
"What did you say?"
"Our parents, do you know why they split?"
"Well, I'm not sure. Perhaps she had too strong a character."
"Or maybe there was someone else?"
"I don't think so. At any rate, Mother didn't remarry."
"But do you always have to remarry after a divorce?"
"Mother never rose higher than department vice head. That's a steep price to pay for a divorce."
"Do you ever imagine that she may have had a relationship with a foreigner ... a Frenchman maybe?"
"During her three months in Paris, you mean?"

"Or perhaps during the war against the French."

"Are you insane? Who would have dared, at that time?"

"..."

"Why do you have these questions all of a sudden?"

"I just feel like I know nothing about our mother."

"The ones who are closest to us are always the ones we pay the least attention to. I don't feel like I know anything about either of them."

"..."

"I have to go. I'll call you when I get to Seoul."

"Looking for a partner for skin-whitening spas and chin-job clinics in Sài Gòn, are you?"

"In the future, perhaps. For the time being, I'm investing in TV dramas, a joint project with the Koreans. The whole world has gone gaga for K-dramas. Me, I prefer beauty contests, life is meant to be a struggle. But we must give the audience what they want, and in this increasingly chaotic society, what they want is serenity. A pinch of romance, a sprinkle of tears, and a thick slice of happy ending. That formula is enough for ninety percent of people to open their wallet."

"..."

"After Seoul, I'm going to Pyongyang. Though that trip doesn't have any practical purpose. It's enough to recall our North in the seventies to know what North Korea is like now. Kim Il Sung's Kumsusan is no different from Uncle Hồ's mausoleum."

"..."

"Can you imagine, guests staying in five-star hotels in the very center of Pyongyang are limited to one hot bath a day. Lack of power. Those days are gone when the Great Leader's portrait was lit up with so many bulbs that Christmas trees would be envious. The North Koreans are all stick thin, which is probably why they adore their leader's cheeks. Genuine adoration, not faked as the West likes to think..."

"..."

"What's the matter with you??"

"Nothing."

"You look so thoughtful."

"I'm listening to your talk."

"I really need to go. I'll call you when I get to Seoul."

"Back when we all lived in the block, you took care of everything around the house, it was you who lined up for vegetables and rice."

"Did I? Even now the North Koreans are still lining up for two hours to buy two grams of China-aid lard."

"You took me to school, you helped me with math, you went to my parent-teacher conferences."

"Your memory is extraordinary. I've long forgotten all that. We're lucky Vietnam didn't become another North Korea."

"My teachers all thought you were my uncle."

"I'm a good twelve years older than you, so that was to be expected. Okay, now I really need to go. I still want to pick something up in the Duty Free."

"..."

"Think about it, will you. What's keeping you in Paris? The thirty-five-hour workweek? Gay marriage? I've long kissed the West goodbye. This is the Asian Century. I'll call you when I get to Seoul."

"..."

25 Paris

Eleven a.m. Victoria was walking a few meters ahead of me, dragging a small cart, the kind you take on grocery trips, but instead of heading to the high street with its shops and supermarkets she turned into a residential area where, at the foot of high-rise buildings, a florist's and a few restaurants flanked a cool pavement shaded by leafy trees. She paused at the florist's, exchanged three euros fifty for a bunch of five yellow roses, then resumed her purposeful gait before stopping short in front of a takeout restaurant. The restaurant was closed, but my target didn't seem surprised, she reached up and pulled the small bell above the door. Today her hand bore only a single ring, one with a ruby-red stone, but her hair was still that wavy, silky-gold perfection. Maybe for every woman there comes a day when the service of a false mane is necessary, I thought.

The door opened just enough for a rotund man to walk out and flash an amiable smile. Victoria nodded slightly and pulled her cart inside, whereupon the door closed. Hovering under an ancient tree nearby, I watched the spots of light wavering on the road and felt the blood congealing within my toes. This morning, after days roaming the city with my brother, I had again dragged myself to the Polotskys' building; like ninety percent of Parisians in July, the couple could go off on holiday at any minute. I had waited for two hours and was feeling desperate when Victoria finally showed up.

I crossed the street toward the takeout restaurant. Stepping behind another tree, concealed from both the sun and my target's line of sight, I tried to imagine what Victoria might be doing beyond that closed door. First, I surmised that she had a young lover, whom she met frequently in the restaurant's basement to make love on a foam mattress above the beaten earth floor. A lot of elderly women, contrary to what you may think, have a very high libido. Then I went on to imagine that she was a longtime member of a secret organization tasked with toppling Moskva's powers that be. Hadn't I witnessed how fervently she had talked about the China-Russia border situation a few days before, in front of the Cathédrale Saint-Alexandre-Nevsky? Finally, I pictured her as a formidable agent in an operation trafficking opium from the former Soviet states. In that cute little cart of hers there might have been a few plastic bags, containing something that looked like cassava flour but had a price tag of hundreds of thousands of dollars. This takeout restaurant was the perfect site for money and goods to change hands: located on the ground floor of a compact forest of high-risers, its back door leads to a veritable labyrinth of stairs and corridors and apartments, enough to defeat even the best informed police ...

The door suddenly flew open, everything inside was illuminated, and a rich, sweet smell permeated the air. One by one, the rotund man slid metal trays bearing all kinds of food into a glass cabinet. Having done with the trays, he hauled Victoria's cart up onto the counter and fished out two bulging plastic bags. I breathed a sigh of relief to see the golden-brown, thickish crêpes that I had recently tasted with black caviar in "Little Russia." This was indeed to be expected. Why shouldn't Victoria supplement her grocery budget with the help of famous delicacies from her husband's homeland? Why shouldn't she indeed, when every home kitchen in the skyscrapers of the 13th arrondissement blazes day and night to furnish the French gourmets with fried nem, salad rolls, stir-fried rice, har gow, sushi ...

The rotund man separated layers of crêpes, arranged them on an oval glass plate, then set the plate in the center of the glass cabinet with an air of deep respect. He looked up at Victoria standing beside him, gave her a rotund thumbs-up, nodded, and again flashed his amiable smile. Shrugging a little and taking the cart back from the man, my target walked swiftly to the door, still holding the bouquet. I was struck by how graceful she looked today, with those yellow roses complementing her golden hair, the ruby-red stone refracting incessant, eerie rays of light of indescribable colors, and in her brown-yellow irises, a sorrow for which there was no word.

I left Victoria in front of her building's gates only to spot her again ten minutes later, on my way to the Métro station, hurriedly getting on a bus.

Unlike what I had imagined as I hastily flagged down a taxi, the car chase I then found myself in wasn't anything like a Hollywood thriller. A few years ago, Paris had joined the exclusive rank of cities that have a dedicated lane for buses and taxis, so rather than frantically weaving through traffic to keep up with Victoria's bus, my taxi had to stop every few minutes each time the bus pulled up at a stop. After about ten stops, my target disembarked. The taxi driver, a Laotian born and bred, was unexpectedly kind and spoke flowing Vietnamese, referring to me as "em" and to himself as "anh"; he gave me his name card and said he would be having lunch in the area in case I needed another ride, or even if I didn't need one, I could just call his "mô bai"; then he winked at me again and hummed, *One day I'll finally know your soul / One day I'll come to you / To say hello ... Vietnam.*

From the bus stop, Victoria walked another three hundred meters or so before turning into a side street. The sun was a furnace. My swollen toes were screaming for a break when my target stopped at the fourth house on the side with even numbers, pushed open the gate and simply walked into the yard.

The moment I glimpsed Victoria getting onto the bus, I had been awed by her efficiency: during the ten minutes it had taken me to get halfway to the Métro station, she had already gone up to her apartment, put away her flowers and cart, changed into a new dress, new heels, new handbag, then descended the stairs to arrive at the stop at the precise moment her bus pulled up.

At one p.m. on a July afternoon, the Parisians were either languidly eating their lunch or languidly taking their siesta (all the curtains were gently snoring) so after twenty minutes the gates still hadn't admitted or released a soul. I could do nothing but stay under the tree and recite to myself for the nth time the dozen signs facing the street: attorney's, dentist's, language class, association of Algerian War veterans . . . coming back again and again to the smallest, most discreet sign, "The Three Smith Brothers—Private Eye Service."

At one thirty, when I had just taken my swollen feet and growling stomach to the other side of the street, Victoria pushed the gates open, holding a large manila envelope. In the middle of the still-deserted street my target silently extracted a sheaf of A4 paper, shrugged and tore them into pieces, then dumped the pieces into a public trash can.

26 Paris

Fifteen minutes later, after I had followed Victoria back to the bus stop and watched her sit down on the bench with my own eyes, I hurried back to the side street. It was with great difficulty that I fished out all the torn fragments, now covered with someone's recent, unfinished lunch, an unappealing mix of tomato sauce, string cheese, minced beef and mayonnaise. I had a few close calls with vomiting, and something told me that this was exactly what my predecessor had been doing while dumping the remains of their meal in the bin.

Nausea gave my empty stomach some hellish cramps. After finding a plastic bag to put the scavenged bits of paper in, I called the Laotian taxi driver. He pulled up after two minutes and promptly asked: "What's the matter with you??" I forced a smile. The driver told me, "What you need like yesterday is something to fill your stomach, how does a hot bowl of phở sound, perhaps tái nạm?" I nodded; not having to walk was a blessing in itself.

The taxi flew down the street, and through half-closed eyes I registered that a few dozen meters away Victoria was standing erect on her high heels, one hand holding her hair in place, the other held up to hail a taxi. I hadn't even had time to cry out before my own taxi slowed down and pulled to the curb: the Laotian driver had spotted my target well before I had, and seemed to be enjoying this detective game. Without a word, he opened the door compartment, held out a pair of sunglasses and gestured at me to put them on, then opened the glove compartment, held out a box of chocolate bars and gestured at me to eat. I put the glasses on, chewed my way through a bar and drank half a bottle of water, until my once-empty stomach had become a water balloon floating inside me, and on my right side there was now a nagging prickling sensation, as if a hyperthin needle was slowly boring into my flesh.

The taxi took off: in front of us, Victoria had gotten into a taxi of her own, a jade-green Peugeot.

Now the Hollywood-style chase that I had anticipated was happening for real. My target seemed in an enormous hurry, she kept glancing at her watch. For a long stretch, our two cars had the bus-and-taxi lane to themselves, and the two drivers performed every trick in their books; the other driver seemed aware of his tail, which made him exhilarated rather than concerned. From afar I could guess that he was getting on in years, with curly salt-and-pepper hair, a trunk like a tree, and muscular shoulders and neck, suggesting someone of North African descent. At times, he let our taxi draw very close and then suddenly shot past an amber light, vanishing into the distance. While the shocked Laotian driver was still letting out a stream of curses, the other car would then reappear, hovering just a few meters in front, taunting and inviting him to resume the chase. But finally, the overexcited taxi pulled too far ahead and we lost track of each other amid the twelve radiating avenues of the Place de l'Étoile, with their tightly woven traffic and cavalier tourists taking pictures in the middle of the street.

After a few minutes of hesitation, the Laotian driver took his chance and dove into avenue Mac-Mahon, only to be promptly held up there by a small construction site where they were fixing a gas pipe. Our quest was looking hopeless when, behind us, a jade-green Peugeot taxi shot into avenue Carnot, and my driver gave a jolly chase until we got close enough to see that the Peugeot carried two men on the back seat and a young woman at the wheel, who wore a high chignon, a back-baring dress, and a most graceful air. The stunned Laotian driver seemed to think hard, and then, perhaps trusting his luck, chose to forge right ahead. But instead of going straight at the crossroads at the end of the avenue he turned left into rue des Acacias, maintaining his speed, then reversed into a decent-sized alley, dodging the cars coming from the opposite direction, at first a few normal-sized cars, then a gigantic moving truck, then a school bus on a day trip, then an ambulance with its shrieking siren which cost him two full minutes of maneuvering, and then we found ourselves in the adjoining street, where Victoria's taxi was hesitating in one place, the driver casting around for a street sign and the passenger gesturing impatiently. When our taxi came into view, that jade-green car visibly shuddered before racing away. The beaming Laotian driver looked at me in the rear mirror and flashed a winning smile; the fare meter was steadily ticking up, and from the car stereo Quynh Anh was still singing: *One day I'll touch your soil / One day I'll finally know your soul …*

The two taxis finally screeched to a halt, simultaneously and about ten meters from each other, on avenue Niel bordering the southwestern banlieue. Victoria got out, not bothering to wait for her change, and hurried away with her head bowed. Her North African driver winked back at his Laotian colleague. I hurried after my target, toes again whining inside toe boxes, the hyperthin needle again prickling my right side. And above my head, the sun was still pouring down its fire.

Victoria went into a bar, "Flowers of the Field," very big and terribly noisy, where she continued straight down to the basement and into a phone booth beside the toilet. I made it into the adjacent booth in time to catch snatches of sentences: "May I talk to Hugo García … Hugo please come, it's only a few minutes' walk … No, I need to see you right this moment … I think it's high time we had a proper talk … I'm gonna wait right here even if I have to wait the whole night… You know what I'm like!" I let out a sigh. If I failed to get to the kindergarten by six, Mike would be taken to the police station.

I wasn't sure how long I'd been napping. After that phone call, Victoria had gone back up the stairs and continued to the second floor, a much quieter space with a single tiny window and dark wallpaper the color of coal smoke, apparently not a favorite among the Flowers clientele. I sat down at a table in a discreet corner, quite far from my target, and wanted to order something to calm the pain in my right side, but the waiters seemed to have forgotten about the existence of this floor, so finally I had put my sunglasses on the table and passed out.

That strange smell was what had woken me up. Over at her table, my target was talking to a man, apparently a good deal younger than her, a tall slender man in a light-colored suit, with ginger hair and a cigar in his hand with its twinkling flame.

"Why this sudden need to see me after all these years?"

"I apologize for calling your office, but it's the only way I have of contacting you. I don't know your mobile number. Back in our day, those staples of civilization hadn't even been dreamed about."

"Are you well? You look tired."

"My doctor urged me to get blood work done again this week. Seems he's seen something in the last one. I sensed that there's something important he hasn't told me yet. What about you? Your aura hasn't dimmed a bit. Must still have that bevy of beauties surrounding you."

"I got divorced, you know."

"I know, and not because you informed me."

"I don't see why I ought to have informed anyone."

"You informed that bevy of beauties surrounding you."

"No, they found out by themselves, just like you."

"What a grandmaster you are."

"Well, you can stay and finish this wine. I need to go. I've got a very important meeting with the chief director."

"With the chief director, or with that bevy of beauties?"

"That's an interesting expression you have. All right, I wish you joy. Send my regards to Paul."

At that, the man got up and walked toward the stairs. Before beginning to descend, he put the cigar between his lips and took a deep drag, then exhaled a soft cloud of smoke through his nose. The air was suddenly filled with that strange fragrance.

I stared as hard as I could at Victoria. The color had drained from her face, her upper lip was quivering, her cheeks were quavering, a lock of blonde hair was trembling loose on her forehead, the ring with the ruby-red stone was shaking on her blue-veined hand that gripped at the wine-puddled tabletop. It was like watching someone caught in an earthquake.

The A4 photographs, pieced together quite successfully though still stinking of stale food, didn't tell me anything new: half of them were of the Countess of Astrakhan in her wide-brimmed hat trailed by Paul Polotsky in the town center of Montrouge; the other half were of Paul Polotsky trailed by Bill in the corridor of the Department of Eastern European Studies. The only surprise was that the camera, whether made in Japan or the PRC, hadn't captured me even once in either of those places. But I also breathed a sigh of relief. To tell the truth, I had no desire to get entangled with those private eyes, the three Smiths who must be as alike as three drops of water, and so dedicated they even saw clients during lunchtime.

27 Paris

Victoria's old flame did indeed have a bevy of beauties surrounding him.

Two days later, once my swollen toes had enjoyed some relief, I decided to return to avenue Niel, hoping to find, if not Hugo García himself, then at least some intel about him from the neighborhood: according to Victoria, "Flowers of the Field" was *only a few minutes' walk* from his office, and he'd worked there for a long time, also according to Victoria, since before the dawn of the era of the cell phone. Generally speaking, whether in Hà Nội or Sài Gòn or Paris, the ladies' man sees his ladies in either a restaurant or a hotel. Of course, if Hugo García was the cautious type he would avoid paying by card or check, to keep his name and home address private. But the man who made Victoria suffer so didn't seem eager to be seen as cautious, but rather as someone who flaunts the *bevy of beauties surrounding him*. He seemed to savor tremendously being the apple of female discord, especially now that he had divorced his wife and was no longer in his prime. What purpose could an autumnal divorce serve for men, if not a chance to enjoy what's left of their virility before giving themselves up to the man's pill and then the nursing home? And because most gentlemen would find it difficult to capitalize on that chance, Hugo García felt he had every right to be proud of himself.

The bow-tied man at the door, who claimed to be the manager of the "Flowers of the Field," shook his head vehemently at the name of Hugo García: "That dude? Look, young lady, I'll be honest with you, don't mention him again if you don't want to see my nasty side. A scoundrel, that's the only word for him. Don't trust him as far as you can throw him, young lady. It's a good job he doesn't show his sorry ass around here anymore. At least not when I'm around."

Five minutes later, I was knocking at the bar next door, where the bartender, perhaps the owner's wife, told me with a shrug that Paul García, Dominique García, Patrick García, and even the famous actor José García, had all graced her establishment, but never had any Hugo García darkened these doors. "Maybe you should try that 'Flowers of the Field.'" She smirked at her own advice. Her thick upturned lips, painted mahogany, were the perfect tableau of two leeches embracing, satisfied after a bloody feast.

I'd made a full round of every single establishment, on both odd- and even-numbered sides of the street, and this in the furious heat of July. "No, we haven't had the honor of serving him." "No, I've been here for years and this is the first time I've heard that name." "No, our chief principle is not to poke into our patrons' affairs." "No, we only keep a blacklist of problem clients." ... That was about the range of answers until I got to the last restaurant, which was as empty as a sad heart: one of the two waiters was annoyed at my interrupting his *so pleasant chitchat* for *such dumb worthless questions*; he also remarked in a barbed tone that agencies must think sleuthing is a piece of cake nowadays, or else they wouldn't employ those *with scant grasp of professional techniques.*

Blood again rushing to my toes, I turned to totter to the door, but the second, older waiter, a short man with a reserved air, followed me and whispered that if the Hugo García I was looking for was a tall sixty-something with ginger hair, quite handsome and never seen without a Havana cigar, I should inquire at the "Blue Waves." He jerked his thumb to indicate a tiny street nearby, then gave me a lingering look of what seemed like genuine compassion.

The "Blue Waves" was at number 30, bustling at three p.m. Its owner seemed to have given up on the name; there was not a single blue or wavy element in the whole restaurant, but there was a gigantic ceramic vase in which climbing roses and grandflower chrysanthemums, both made of satin, were not so much arranged as randomly flopped in. It took me twenty minutes to secure a small table near the entrance. As revenge, I splurged on a bottle of iced lemonade, spaghetti with stir-fried chicken and greens, and a crème brûlée with raspberry sauce. My instinct told me that Hugo García must be somewhere near at hand, so I could take my time and treat my stomach to some decent nourishment, my poor stomach that had been constantly abused this past week: full to the point of bursting when Mai had been here, and then empty to the point of pain.

The roar of the clientele was deafening and the rush of the waiters was dizzying and the grotesqueness of the fake flowers was eye-assaulting, but the food was good, the AC was generous, and it was simply heaven to be able to finally sit on a chair (with a cool leather seat and wooden armrests) and look out of the window at the misery outside: those dried-up trees, those sweat-drenched people. It felt like Sài Gòn had temporarily lent its sky to Paris. Once I had drained the lemonade and polished off the spaghetti, I noticed in one corner of the room a flight of wooden stairs that led to the basement, a basement that was perhaps reserved for the regulars as the stairs were well hidden behind the bar, which in turn was hidden behind that grotesque flower arrangement.

I descended the stairs and, beneath the basement waiter's astonished gaze, walked right into the strange fragrance from the day before: in the middle of the room, Hugo García was puffing on his cigar as he poured his heart out into his cell phone: "I'm getting weary now, my man, you get how it is. My girls are so needy. Not to mention such a drain on my wallet. And I was a bad student at the school of frugality. Perhaps I need to settle down with one of them. No, nothing of that marriage nonsense, but I need to settle down, my man, you understand how it is. But she needs a shapely pair of legs, no compromise on that."

I sat down in the chair across from him at the very moment

he was barking a string of "hello?" into the phone. Still mentally immersed in the unexpectedly interrupted conversation, he just nodded mechanically when I uttered the name "Victoria," then paused for a moment before bursting into laughter:

"But which Victoria, pray? Shulz? Dubois? Or perhaps Delaporte?"

Before I could answer, he continued gaily:

"Here's a pro tip: women named Victoria are often overendowed with complications and underendowed in the leg department."

It seemed that the tearful reunion in the "Flowers of the Field" only the day before hadn't left so much as a scratch on his mind.

"Victoria Polotsky!"

"The wife of that Paul?"

I eagerly nodded. But his expression had already changed: his gregariousness had given way to a suspicious stare, so I had to give him a digested version of Bill's story, adding that Bill was now in such despair that he would lose the will to live if he can't learn the truth, furthermore that Bill was a true friend of mine who I would naturally hate to see wither away. I must have sounded convincing enough, because Hugo García just said with a shrug:

"I never heard anything about Paul having a son out of wedlock. Victoria has never said anything to me, perhaps she doesn't know herself, or doesn't want to."

The cigar in his hand was twinkling in the dim light of the basement. Suddenly he smoothed his hair with the other hand and suggested:

"Girl, if you have the time, stay and quench your thirst with me."

I nodded. It wasn't such a bad idea. This character in front of me was worth further investigation. And my toes were still recovering from the most recent trek.

Hugo García and I shared a large, chilled bottle of beer, the finest beer from Alsace. I made quick work of my glass, while he had to put his down again and again to answer phone calls, all but one from women, in which he chirruped away, giving and receiving "my sweetest kisses," but the longest call was from a man, the one he had been talking to when interrupted. Hugo García showered *my man* with his *most intimate thoughts* as casually as if I hadn't been there, and those thoughts all converged on the single topic of *a shapely pair of legs, to settle or not to settle?* After promising to beam over photos of those shapely legs for the approval of *my man,* he turned off his phone, shook his head at me in lieu of an apology and, glancing at his watch, said he was all mine now, for whatever questions *you girl* might need to ask, about Victoria or Paul or both of them, as long as I did it in ten minutes sharp, because he had a very important meeting with the chief director.

Ten minutes, I told myself, seemed to be the number favored by big shots and countesses alike.

"What organization does Paul Polotsky serve in?"

"He had many jobs, but he was never a spy!"

I fixed my eyes on him, but Hugo García just shrugged:

"Why sweat such trivial things. Your young friend should know that having a priest or an executioner for a father wouldn't add or subtract one bit from his own worth. Take me for example, I didn't give a rat's ass who my daddy was or what he did, it would just add unnecessary complications to my life. If the old shit had been a president or a billionaire, the newshounds would sniff me out in no time, you can be sure of that. And if it had been the other way around, well, paternal love is always costly. I haven't worked my ass off to sink my loot into a nursing home …"

"Was Paul Polotsky ever in Indochina?"

"How many pulp novels must have you been reading! Why would Paul want to go gadding about those war-torn places of yours?"

I had to clutch at the armrests to keep from falling off my chair.

"Believe me, girl, it's the truth! I've known Paul since he was a snotty urchin!"

I said nothing. That last statement must be true given that he told Victoria so nonchalantly to *send my regards to Paul.* I glanced at my watch, thinking that if only I had another ten minutes, I would surely get to the bottom of this fascinating love triangle; I still remembered how all the color had drained from Victoria's face the day before, on the second floor of "Flowers of the Field," backed by wallpaper the color of coal smoke, above a tabletop puddled with spilt wine.

"Did he ever live at number 21 avenue de Suffren?"

With a mischievous smile, Hugo García took a name card from his chest pocket, wrote down his mobile phone number and winked at me:

"Girl, that question will have to wait for another day."

He had just handed the card to me when a woman's voice practically shook the basement: "Got you now! Your number is always busy. I called your office and they said you were in an important meeting. But I just knew that you would be here!" He hadn't had time to answer when a pair of Scarlett Johansson–caliber legs found their way into his lap, and a pair of arms no less shapely twined around his neck.

Every step of the ascent sent a throbbing pain through my spine. My toes have really given up the ghost, I thought, slumping against the wall. The beautiful wooden stairs had no banister. I was seeing stars. From the ground floor, a young woman's voice was trilling: "Hugo please come ... I'm gonna wait right here even if I have to wait the whole night ... You know what I'm like ..." I suspected that this was another specimen from his collection of Victorias, and would very much have liked to have a glance at her, but the restaurant was bustling at four p.m., over half of the patrons were female, and not all of them wearing the kind of outfit that would allow me to verify the accuracy of his statement about *women named Victoria being underendowed in the leg department.*

28 Paris

Mr. Điền lived in the 5th arrondissement, in the Latin Quarter, across the street from a little park whose baby fountain, trying to copy the adults, was having its own July holiday.

I don't know how long I would've been sitting on that park bench if the gates hadn't suddenly flung open and Mr. Điền himself walked out, not alone but side by side with a slender woman, dark hair and white dress, who looked quite young as far as I could tell from behind.

I sighed; so this was why he hadn't touched his phone since last night. After a few moments of deliberation, I decided to follow them, hoping for an opportunity to remind him of his promise to *go find an old friend of my mother when I had time.*

Mr. Điền and the woman went in the direction of boulevard Saint-Michel. Today he wore light-colored clothes and sneakers but seemed even older and more emaciated, and even from afar his face was a spiderweb of wrinkles, the brand-name sunglasses losing their battle with his crow's feet. When they reached the boulevard, Mr. Điền invitingly pointed to a small café but the woman shook her head; they both looked down at the ground, exchanged a few words, and then he stepped into the street and waved to a taxi on the prowl at the crossroads ahead. One left, one stayed. It was over in a minute and not a tear was shed. But the scene had given me the impression of a heartbreaking farewell.

Old Mr. Điền and I were left alone on the pavement, ten meters apart, of the abruptly uncharacteristically serene boulevard. After a few minutes of hesitation, he turned and went into the café he'd pointed to. Silently I followed. The spacious room didn't have a single patron. The owner, working on his computer at the bar, looked up to greet Mr. Điền and then cast an inquiring glance at me. Mr. Điền just walked over in silence to a table by the window. He sat down, pointed to the chair across from his and said, without greeting or even turning to look at me: "Wouldn't want to let me know you'd come, would you."

A long hour of silence stretched between my one-time neighbor and me, as we faced each other over two coffees that remained untouched. I gave it another five minutes, then, taking a gulp of the now cold and bitter coffee, I told him I still remembered what he had said in the floating restaurant concerning *an old friend of my mother*. I had to repeat it twice before Mr. Điền seemed to jolt awake. He said:

"Your mother's old friend—on the very first day I arrived in Paris I went to look for him, I sat for hours in all kinds of public transportation. Number 21 avenue de Suffren was where it should be, but Paul Polotsky was not. No one I asked had ever heard of that name. Only after a while did I learn that the civilized world has invented such a thing as a phone book, in which I patiently searched, through Paris and the twenty-four regions of France, and arrived at a list of ten Polotskys. Only after a while longer did I have money enough for a 120-unit phone card and a good enough command of French to make use of it. Four p.m. every Sunday, when Frenchmen and women emerge from their lunch and nap, I would go to a public phone booth and dial a number on the list, hoping to reach someone related to Paul Polotsky. I don't remember how many cards I used up before I got to the end of that list, because every Sunday I would end up talking to an elderly person tormented by a lifetime of memories. Finally, just when I was about to despair, this one call happened:

"'Please can you tell me if this is Mr. Paul Polotsky's residence?'

"'He's not home. Who's this?'

"'Please, I have something important to discuss with Mr. Paul Polotsky.'

"'You can ask me. I'm his wife.'

"'I'm sorry, I need to speak to Mr. Polotsky directly.'

"'Are you from the organization?'

"'I don't understand.'

"'You'd better own up right away, you're liaising with Paul to assign him a task, right?'

"'What kind of task?'

"'Don't pretend you're an idiot. The task your side is charged with is to topple our side to the ground, then to march into Paris and after that right on to Washington. That's what the media calls the cold war, right?'

"'When will Mr. Paul Polotsky be at home? To tell you the truth, I'm fed up with this questioning.'

"'You tell that organization of yours that I'm his wife, I know everything, and I am against this, because it threatens my husband's safety and by extension my own.'

"'But what organization, for goodness's sake?'

"Every time I thought back to this phone call, I wondered why the woman hung up right after my final question, and then the line went busy and the following day the number went dead. A few years ago I tried the number again, but was still met with the operator's voice."

After he'd finished, Mr. Điền resumed staring at the wall in silence. Outside, the rain was coming down. Inside, the café was filling up. At the next table, a couple were writhing together in full rain gear, sending their own mini downpour splashing everywhere. I couldn't tell exactly what was going on inside me. But most prominent was overwhelming bewilderment. How could my mother have told Mr. Điền about Paul Polotsky? I'd thought she had kept him utterly secret, to be taken to her grave, never a word breathed to another.

Mr. Điền stood up without a word and left, leaving me behind with my bewilderment. Later, in the Métro, I managed to get lost twice, first boarding a train going in the wrong direction and then forgetting to get out at Place d'Italie. For the whole afternoon my mind grappled with that one question: how could my mother have told Mr. Điền about Paul Polotsky? I'd always thought that to him, our former neighbor, she'd only ever played the role of deputy head of the local civil unit.

For the whole afternoon I sat motionless in Madame Wang's crafts shop. No customer came in, no sudden downpour arrived to distract me, however temporarily, from that mother-shaped question.

Fifteen minutes before I closed the shop for the day, I began to visualize the following scene: shortly after my parents' divorce, on a winter afternoon when the cold was as sharp as a knife, when not a soul was to be seen on the third-floor corridor, my mother had invited Mr. Điền over. Under his surprised and somewhat apprehensive gaze, my mother gently closed the door and lowered her voice:

"Mr. Điền, my good neighbor, I have an important favor to ask you, a very important thing that I couldn't count on anyone else for."

Mr. Điền was so moved by these words that his eyes became dewy:

"Please tell me, and I'll try my best to help you. In my workplace there is no side project, and the benefits are miserable, but if someone you know has a kid newly graduated and looking for a job, I think I can . . ."

My mother hurriedly shook her head, interrupting him:

"Any kid looking for a job can just keep looking, I won't have anything to do with it."

The apprehension crept back into Mr. Điền's gaze. My mother lowered her voice almost to a whisper:

"Can you do me this favor—on your way to Cuba, if you decide to stay in France—can you please contact this old friend of mine ..."

At that, she stopped to gauge Mr. Điền's reaction, who now seemed petrified. A few minutes later, still not having recovered his wits, he waved his hand in denial:

"Who told you that I would stay in France?"

My mother, still whispering:

"No one told me, I just guessed."

Mr. Điền, trembling like a leaf:

"If you tell the police, you may as well kill me."

My mother was silent. Her silence made him tremble all the more. When he couldn't bear it anymore, he said abjectly:

"What's your old friend's name? What's the address?"

Only then did my mother take from her pocket a slip of paper with Paul Polotsky's name and address already written on it, and asked Mr. Điền to learn these by heart then and there. It was a piece of cake for someone who was used to dealing with the chemical recipes of food, so the trembling Mr. Điền passed that test with flying colors. After grilling him again and again to make sure that the information was carved into his memory, my mother tore up the slip of paper and told him to depart with peace of mind, his trip would be smooth as butter. Mr. Điền breathed out with relief; he seemed to understand the bargain now, and asked her:

"And what should I say to this old friend?"

Now it was my mother's turn to tremble. She looked out of the door in silence. There was still not a soul to be seen on the third-floor corridor. The cold was still a cutting knife. After a while, to Mr. Điền's wide-eyed astonishment, she said:

"Please tell Paul that whatever happens, I'll never forget him."

This, Mr. Điền could remember even without my mother's bidding. He was silent. So was she. The two of them sat in silence until they began to hear footsteps out in the corridor.

In the days that followed, it was as if nothing had happened between them. The morning when he departed, she ran into him in the corridor, whether deliberately or not, and instantly assumed the role of the civil unit's deputy head: "Mr. Điền, please work well in our brotherly country with peace of mind. Should your wife and little Liên run into any trouble, our block will do our best to help!" Flustered, Mr. Điền expressed his gratitude to the block. Maybe he also wanted some role to perform but couldn't think of one in time. My mother cast another look at him, then turned and left.

I went to bed very late, expecting a night of insomnia. Around five in the morning I had a strange dream, in which I saw a room, narrow and dark, a 1977 calendar on the wall, my mother sitting in a remote corner, behind a pile of phone books listing numbers from Paris and the twenty-four regions of France. I could hear her heart thumping. At first I thought it was nerves. Then I thought maybe it was fear: at any moment Madame Hòa or the embassy staff could rush in, and their eyes would bulge at the list she was holding of thirteen Mr. Polotskys. I struggled for a few minutes and was about to wake up when I sank instead into a new dream. This time I saw a phone booth, tiny but complete with glass walls and fluorescent lights, my mother standing erect inside, holding the receiver in one hand and dialing with the other, then bursting out the moment the call had connected: "Please can you tell me if this is Mr. Paul Polotsky's residence?" And she kept repeating that same sentence in varying tones of voice, no matter what the voice on the other end responded, until she hung up exhausted, but then immediately picked the receiver up again to dial another number, and so on and so forth until she had used up a whole 120-unit phone card, the equivalent of a week's stipend granted to Vietnamese fellows in France.

I woke up and thought in a daze that if Mr. Điền, who had

arrived years later, could track down Paul Polotsky's number from the phone books, then my mother might well also have discovered it during her three months in Paris, at one of those rare times when Madame Hòa got a headache that sent her to bed early or was busy snooping on Mrs. Huệ. My mother had found his number and attempted contact, fully aware that if their liaison was exposed she would be counted twice as guilty as Mrs. Huệ. And she didn't discount the possibility of being escorted to the airport by the Embassy's top security officer and sent home on the next flight available. Trembling, she had dialed the number. Trembling, Polotsky had answered. And then they may well have met in a secret attic room the way Kai and I did, and made love on the wooden floor the way Kai and I did, looked at each other's face solemnly the way Kai and I did, and parted in silence the way Kai and I did...

Kai had told me that whatever happened he wouldn't forget me. My mother had wanted to tell Polotsky that whatever happened she wouldn't forget him.

29 Paris

The last day before the summer holiday, the Vietnamese language class couldn't conclude without that comment about *a bite after this.*

After we were all settled down in the restaurant (the same one as last time, because that clay pot-steamed chicken simply had to be tasted), the most studious woman of the class ceremoniously presented to me a neat pretty box, wrapped in patterned paper, and even tied with a bow. I opened it to find a trio of Transformer robots inside. I said, thank you all, on behalf of Mike. Everybody clapped in delight. Today, for some unknown reason, both Ms. Rhino and Mr. Bullfrog were absent, but *that dude Luc* was there in their stead: when everybody was getting ready to leave, he had simply tagged along, unabashed, but no one paid any heed, and then at the restaurant he had taken a seat, still unabashed, and still no one paid any heed and he got away with it. After orders were placed, someone loudly sang the praises of Mr. Bullfrog's previous generosity. A few joined the chorus. But another said: "Generosity my ass, he took that bill back to his company!" Stunned, the others looked at one another without further commentary. I recognized the voice of the stung man I had overheard in the Métro.

The rambunctious classmates were egging Luc on to eat the fat pygostyle in his bowl when a ringing sound came from my handbag. A man's voice said he needed to see me right away, *for a very important matter*. Panicked, I cried into the phone: "Where's Mike?" The man was silent. I pressed him: "Which hospital did they take him to?" Still the man said nothing. No time to explain to my students; I grabbed my bag and ran outside.

When I was already in a taxi speeding towards the 13th arrondissement, my phone rang a second time, this time somehow from my coat pocket. Penetrating through the swishing wind in my ear, the same man's voice repeated that he needed to see me right now, *for a very important matter*. I doubled up, unable to speak. In my mind I had already seen my neighbor's house going up in flames, firefighters rushing in to search every corner but finding no trace of Mike. The man's voice added that if I didn't mind, he would come to my place and we could talk there. I stammered: "Where is Mike?" but only heard a beeping sound in reply: the connection had been lost in the speeding car. Various scenarios played out in my mind in rapid succession: Mike had watched TV while eating so he'd choked on a bone and was now lying in a heap on the floor; Mike had grabbed the Transformer robot from my neighbor's nephew so the other kid beat him up and split his head open; Mike had played soccer on the balcony and fell down seven floors ...

I flew out of the elevator. My neighbor was already waiting outside his door, holding Mike's hand; he shook his head and told me this was the last time he would agree to look after my kid, who took as much looking after as ten other children put together. Then the door slammed shut.

My phone rang for the umpteenth time, and it took me an inhumanly long time to find it in the bathroom, where I had spent a terribly long time cleansing myself under the shower, after putting Mike to bed and turning off all the lights. That man's voice informed me that he had been standing in the corridor for a good hour, waiting for me to open the door. I drew back the latch, a butcher's knife ready in my hand.

The door had only opened a crack when I recognized Bill. He regarded my knife with perfect calm. In the corridor's glaring light I saw how wrecked his face looked, and wondered why the wrinkles had conducted such an assault on him, then, correcting myself, thought that at any rate this version of him still looked more pleasant than the plaster statue. He asked for my permission to come in.

He spoke now slowly and ruefully, a world apart from the monotonous, detached voice of a few weeks back. When I noticed a mosquito in the small glass of water on the table, Bill was whispering that the *very important matter* he had been anxious to tell me about was that his birth father wasn't our Paul Polotsky. To my wide-eyed astonishment, he whispered that his father was a different Paul Polotsky, not the Eastern European Studies professor that both he and I had been doggedly tailing separately, a piece of information that had only come to light two hours ago, upon which he had called me immediately.

"I decided to seek the help of a professional detective. I told him my story, and that I was now in such despair, I'd lost my will to live if I couldn't learn the truth. He gave it some thought, then asked for seven days to do what he does. It was the longest week I ever lived through. I couldn't eat. I couldn't sleep. But the detective made good on his promise. At five p.m. today he called me and asked me to come to his office. I was so nervous, my teeth were clattering when I greeted him. The first thing he said was to offer me his deepest condolences. I didn't understand at all. What condolences, and why. He looked me straight in the eye and said in a low voice that my birth father, Paul Polotsky, born in 1935 in Saint Petersburg, had migrated to France during the Second World War and passed away forty years ago. It was a huge shock. The ground seemed to tremble beneath my feet. Incredibly, my father had died the very year I was born. When I'd recovered enough to speak, I asked the detective about the cause of death, which I guessed had been sudden. He took an envelope from his drawer and asked if I had the heart to look at these things. I nodded, and told him I was ready to learn the truth. Without a word he handed me a dozen photos of a violent traffic accident; all that was left at the site was a blackened car frame; my father's body and everything inside the car had turned to ash. Watching my dejected face, the detective said that according to the traffic cops' files, the victim had been driving on the southern highway, twenty-two kilometers from Lyon. My heart pained to hear it; my mother's parents were Lyonnaise; for all we know my parents had met in that city; for all we know my father, even though he hadn't maintained contact, had heard about my birth and was coming to visit us. If the car hadn't burnt to ashes, perhaps we would've known what it was transporting; there even could have been suitcases of toys and baby clothes. Finally, I said I wanted to know how he had looked when he was alive, and every piece of information that the detective had managed to gather. He handed me a large photo, apparently a yearbook photo, showing around twenty high school students standing in three rows. I skimmed through the faces and stopped at a young man in a long overcoat, with dark hair and melancholic, limpid eyes, so limpid that if the rest of him had been blotted out I would have thought them a child's. He himself seemed to be looking at me intently, as though there was something he wanted to tell me. I felt within me the beginning of tears. I looked up, and the detective nodded. That was my father all right, a few months before he died, with his students at a high school in a Parisian banlieue. 'Your father was an amateur practitioner of the theatrical art and also an adventurer, he had gone as far as Indochina by the time he was nineteen.' Before I left, the detective gave me that photo and a play script, saying these copies had been made especially for me. He saw me to the door and said that at least there was a silver lining in this, that my mind would be at ease now, because the Paul Polotsky I'd talked to on the phone twenty years ago and had been stalking for the last few months was definitively not my father. The detective had conducted an extensive investigation, even acquiring the other Paul Polotsky's medical history, so he could say with absolute certainty that the other Paul Polotsky was both incurably sterile and incurably delusional. I left as if in a trance, not saying goodbye to the detective. I don't believe my mind will be at ease. I don't believe my heart will be free of its burden. For the last twenty years, my first thought in the morning has always been to wonder if this is what paternal love is like. For the last twenty years, I've been living in doubt. And when I discovered the truth, I discovered something else: for the last twenty years, I've actually been longing for death."

Bill was sobbing. I cast a quick glance at the large photo in his hand and immediately recognized the face from the black-and-white photo my mother had hidden inside the cover of her notebook.

Bill was still sobbing. Perhaps Paul Polotsky's delusion had infected not only the two women by his side, namely Victoria and the Countess of Astrakhan, but also caused Bill (who had merely spoken to him briefly over the phone) to go mad over what people call paternal love.

I was suddenly reminded of my own strange phone call, when the person on the other end had suspected me of working for the Chinese immigrant mafia, tasked with recovering the title deeds of the four islands to the east of the Amur that the Tsar had given to the Qing dynasty for a song, a century ago. Perhaps my interlocutor had been some naïve member of the Polotsky clan, who'd also contracted delusions from Paul. Then I considered that maybe this delusion of his, left untreated for too long, had come to the terminal stage. For too long, Paul Polotsky had thought of himself as serving some secret organization, working on the noblest jobs. For too long, he had been playing hide-and-seek with his telephone, disappearing for years at a time to thwart anyone who wanted to track him down.

I wondered if I should tell Bill that the walking directory of the Russian expat community had also once met a Paul Polotsky, a bachelor and a amateur playwright, a high school teacher in a Parisian banlieue, who perished in a traffic accident in the 1960s.

Suddenly there was a knock at the door. Young Luc timidly poked his head in, holding the box of Transformer robots I had left at the restaurant. He apologized for showing up without calling first. After I had rushed away in the taxi, my students had left the clay pot-steamed chicken untasted while they telephoned every single hospital in Paris to find out which emergency room Mike had been admitted to, before ascertaining with relief that nowhere had a patient with the name Mike Nguyen. And since everyone else needed to leave for their holiday early the next day, young Luc had volunteered to bring the box to my door. He'd found my address as soon as he looked it up in the phone book. Smiling an amused smile, he told me that in the whole of France there is not another name as odd as mine. Finally, he confided that he hadn't called first because he'd been afraid that I would tell him not to come, and that if I hadn't opened the door, he had intended to just leave the box in the corridor, probably no one would have the heart to throw Mike's Transformers into the trash can. Young Luc had many more things to confide. He was planted on my threshold, one foot in, one foot out. Perhaps this was the first time he'd been able to confide in me freely without fear of being taunted or given the evil eye by his classmates. He kept hold of the box, didn't give it to me right away. He seemed emotional. He stammered.

Bill slipped out of the apartment by ducking easily under the arm of young Luc, who was a good head taller than him. Only when the elevator slammed shut did I push Luc aside to run out to the corridor. Flustered, he apologized, pressed the box into my hands and then left, not taking the elevator but opening the door to the emergency staircase. He seemed to know this block even better than me.

30 Paris

I didn't go back inside right away but stood there with my back against the wall. The corridor was empty. After a few seconds, the lights went out, and I stayed there in the fathomless dark. I felt as though my feet, which had become deformed after so many days traipsing across Paris, were rooted to the spot. I had spent six endless months pursuing a goal that a professional detective had accomplished in a week, and if Bill hadn't come to inform me, perhaps tomorrow, and the day after tomorrow, and the days after that, I would have continued dragging myself to Paul Polotsky's building, nervously trailing my target, my target's wife, or anyone who happened to cross their paths.

That my Paul Polotsky might have passed away was something I'd never considered. And neither had my mother. I imagined how during her three-month fellowship in France, navigating Madame Hòa's iron grip, she had slipped out of the Vietnamese embassy, patiently searched through the phone books of Paris and the twenty-four regions of France to arrive at a list of over ten Polotskys, then patiently called every single one. She was fully aware that if their liaison was exposed, she would be counted twice as guilty as Mrs. Huệ. And she didn't discount the possibility of being escorted to the airport by the embassy's top security officer and sent home on the next flight available. But still she patiently called the numbers, one after the other. Perhaps at some point she'd stumbled upon the delusional Paul Polotsky. Their brief conversation would have gone thus:

"Please can you tell me if this is Mr. Paul Polotsky's residence?"

"Who do I have the honor of conversing with?"

"I don't know if you still remember me, but we met over twenty years ago, in Hà Nội, in Hỏa Lò prison, where I was imprisoned by your government ..."

"What is this? What reason did they have to put you in prison? I hope they didn't torture you too brutally, and that our agents arrived in time to liberate you."

"Please don't be so modest, it was thanks to you and your uncle's intervention that I was released on the third day."

"No, no, don't say so, we only acted on the instructions of our organization."

"We had such a wonderful night together. Do you remember?"

"Yes, yes, our agents always know how to handle things perfectly."

"I still have the photo you gave me."

"What photo?"

My mother hung up, dejected. Paul Polotsky had forgotten everything. Leaning against the wall of the phone booth, she let loose a torrent of tears. Someone banged on the door and told her to go cry somewhere else so others could use the phone. She left, crying as she walked. She was still crying when she saw Madame Hòa standing arms folded in front of the embassy, her face a picture of anger. My mother trembled. Fortunately, Madame Hòa was keeping an eye out for Mrs. Huệ, and took no notice of my mother's swollen eyes. That night, my mother's pillow was soaked with tears. Perhaps the following nights were the same. But then, life went on. Until the plane soared away, taking them from Paris, and she burst into tears again. Fortunately, Madame Hòa was still keeping both eyes on Mrs. Huệ and took no notice of my mother's sobs. She was crying when the plane landed at Moskva. She cried throughout the journey on the transnational train. Central Asia, Siberia, Mongolia, Beijing ... nothing could dry her tears. She cried until she saw my father waiting, arms folded, at Hàng Cỏ station, his face a picture of glee. My mother trembled. Fortunately, my father only had eyes for the scooter and the copper bicycle with the Peugeot labels, and took no notice of my mother's swollen eyes. That night, her pillow was soaked with tears. Perhaps the following nights were the same. But then, life went on. Until the bone-chilling winter took over Hà Nội, and my mother burst into tears again. Fortunately, my father was busy lobbying for the vice directorship of that university in Ho Chi Minh City and took no notice of her sobs. Her pillow didn't even have time to dry before it got soaked again. Until the day my parents took each other to court. Until the sudden news that Mr. Điền was departing for Cuba to study how to make sugar from sugarcane, on a convoluted journey but with one stopover in Paris to replenish the plane's stock of fuel and baguettes. That night, wrapping herself in the cotton blanket, she decided to stop crying and calmly rethink her conversation with Paul Polotsky. By the time dawn drew near and roosters began to crow, she had come up with three possible reasons to explain Paul Polotsky's forgetfulness.

One: there was someone else with him when she called, perhaps even his wife with her thigh across his.

Two: he'd had some alcohol in his system, perhaps even a full liter-and-a-half bottle of vodka.

Three: he had been half-asleep, perhaps not even aware of what he was saying.

All three were highly plausible, especially as his voice had been totally changed from what she remembered from their encounter in Hỏa Lò.

Please tell Paul that whatever happens, I'll never forget him. She risked everything in asking Mr. Điền to pass on those words.

After Mr. Điền left, she began to wait for news from France. The news that Mr. Điền had become a *loose bike chain,* a source of great agony for his wife, was a source of equally great hope for my mother. Patiently she watched for news from France. Day after day. Month after month.

Year after year went by.

Until the year 2004. That night of torrential rain. In an alien city. I couldn't help but picture the way she would have fallen from the top floor to the ground floor, in the dark tunnellike space of that elevator in Sài Gòn. I couldn't help but think that she had chosen her death.

Half a century leading to a death. To the day. Since that fateful encounter in Hỏa Lò prison between my mother and a certain Paul Polotsky.